BED, BREAKFAST & BONES

By Carolyn L. Dean

Visit the author at http://www.CarolynDeanBooks.com

BED, BREAKFAST & BONES is copyright 2016 by Carolyn L. Dean. All rights reserved. This book or any portion thereof may not be reproduced or used in any manner whatsoever without the express written permission of the author or publisher, except for the use of brief quotations in critical articles or reviews.

DEDICATION:

For my **first and my last**, and for my parents, **Carol** and **Dean**.

For the world's greatest beta readers! **Beth, Eric, Geri, Jeff, Nancy, Sharon, Spencer, and Viktoria.**

And again, for **Spencer**, my good friend and writing buddy, who made sure I got this done.

D0720296

It was easy to find Mrs. Granger inside the general store, and Meg had been spot on when she described her as Yoda. She was a little cotton-haired lady of indeterminate age and shape, sitting on a padded wooden bench near an antique stove, her four-wheeled walker parked close by. Quietly knitting fingerless gloves by the light of the large window next to her, she was obviously eavesdropping on the lively conversation at the checkout register ten feet away.

"Mrs. Granger?" Amanda asked. She held the pink cinnamon roll box in her hands, waiting.

"Shhhhh! Just a minute..."

Amanda shifted foot to foot while the checker wrapped up her conversation with the chatty customer, and thanked her as she headed out the door.

With a satisfied sigh, the old lady settled back on the bench. "Now, what can I do for you, dear?"

Amanda held out the box. "Meg said I should come talk to you, and she sent over some pastries."

The toady little woman's eyes lit up, and she made excited "ooo" sounds as she grabbed the box.

"Have a seat!" She gestured vaguely at the wooden bench next to her as she pried open the lid and dug into the fat cinnamon roll.

"Sorry to shush you, but I was listening to Mary Anne Bates tell Myrna about her new Chrysler." Her voice dropped to a conspiratorial whisper. "You know, she's not a bad person, except she forgets to vote and she does grow the marijuana down in her chicken shed." Mrs. Granger pulled a huge piece of icing off the top of the roll and waved it at Amanda. "I don't like that. It's not healthy," she said, as she expertly crammed the chunk of frosting into her mouth.

After a couple minutes of enthusiastic chewing, she came up for air and smiled at Amanda. "You're the lady with the problem buried under her scarecrow, or rather, the problem that *was* buried under your scarecrow."

"You know about that?"

"Oh honey, I read the paper like a good taxpayer should. I'm figurin' you probably came to ask me about how Emmett wound up in your garden, six feet under."

"Um, it was more like three."

"Whatever."

Table of Contents

Chapter 1

"I'd burn it to the ground."

Amanda Graham swiveled her head toward her friend, incredulous.

"You'd *what*?"

Beth's voice was determined and serious. "Burn it. All of it. One lit match, a couple of gallons of kerosene and WHOOSH. A lovely empty lot to sell. With an ocean view."

Amanda took a long, hard look at the abandoned Ravenwood Inn, huge and empty for years. It sprawled across the shaded lawn like the bleached skeleton of a once-fine debutante, left to rot after a long history of visiting friends and elegant parties. Every line of its Victorian frame, the wide porches and gingerbread details on the many balconies, showed that it had once been loved in this little coastal town. If she used her imagination a bit, she could almost hear the laughter and see the ghosts of the previous guests as they walked arm in arm up the broad front steps, decked out in their finest evening attire from decades past.

"Some of it's brick. It wouldn't burn well anyway," she said, being practical. Maybe she was looking at the situation with rose-colored glasses, but her mind was made up. If she was going to live here, she was going to have to look past the peeling paint and boarded up windows.

"I think it just needs some work and it could be amazing. You know, for years this used to be the most popular bed and breakfast in the area. It's probably had hundreds of guests visit here. Everyone knew the Ravenwood Inn."

Beth looked skeptical. "What, a hundred years ago? A thousand?" She laid a gentle hand on her friend's shoulder, but her words were brutally honest.

"You're not up to this, Amanda, and you know it. This thing's a money pit, and to fix it up will take every last dime you made from the sale of your condo. I understand you have some weird family attachment to it, but you need to be practical."

Just the mention of the condo's sale gave Amanda a stab of pain. She wasn't sorry she sold that place after her boyfriend Ken had left her, but the whole thing had been so sordid and awful that she'd known she needed a brand new life. When she got the word that her last living relative, her uncle Conrad, had died and left her Ravenwood Inn, she'd been both stunned and relieved. Maybe it was a sign that her need for a new life and a different place to live was coming true. Perhaps she could reinvent herself in this little town.

"I'm tired of being practical, Beth. I've been practical my whole life. I'm tired of having everything planned out and people telling me what to do and bad, stupid men. I need a new start, and what better place to do it than in a small Oregon beach town off the beaten path?"

Beth snorted, unimpressed. "You mean Hicksville."

Amanda looked around at the quiet country road lined with snug cottages surrounded by neatly-trimmed flower beds. The narrow road was quiet and empty. Behind the inn the weak autumn sun was already setting, making the long shadows of early evening slide under the huge trees in the front yard.

"Maybe, but I might as well build a new life here in Hicksville as anywhere else."

She heard a sharp huff of annoyance behind her and turned to see a plump local matron glare disapprovingly at them as she hurried away, clutching her oversized purse.

Great. An excellent start with a possible neighbor, she thought. *Just what I need.*

She turned back to her friend, ignoring the sudden gust of cool wind swirling through her thin sweatshirt. "I appreciate you coming up here with me, Beth, and I know you want what's best for me. The truth is that I need something new, and I think this could be it. Nobody knows me here and no one knows what happened. I can start fresh. They don't need to know anything about me except that I now own a cool, old hotel."

She gestured to the silent, unlit inn again. "This is my chance at a clean, boring, mundane life, and I'm going to take it."

It was a heartfelt speech, but she wasn't surprised when her friend dug in her purse and pulled out her car keys.

"Call me when you're desperate for sushi and civilization again, girlfriend. I'll come running." Her voice sounded almost pitying. She kissed Amanda on the cheek and gave her a last, tight hug. "It'll be getting dark soon, and I don't want to be driving home too late. Let me know if you need anything," she said, and headed toward her car.

It took almost two minutes of effort to make the rust-pocked key turn in the lock set in Ravenwood Inn's massive front door. Amanda was careful not to push too hard on the elaborate leaded glass insert when she muscled the door open wide enough to squeeze inside.

From what she could see in the fading light the front entry hall was enormous, strung with huge, looping cobwebs like some forgotten party streamers. She clicked on her flashlight and could just make out a large chandelier above her head and a curved staircase right in front of her. Wide, arched doorways on her right and left led into dark, silent rooms, and she could barely see the shapes of abandoned furniture. The air was stale and dry, as if the inn had been sealed for years and she was the first living thing inside it again. She shivered, her eyes surveying the entrance quickly, trying to still her thumping heart and see everything at once. Amanda half-expected some long-sleeping ghost to waft in and greet her, and then request to see her reservation before she was able to check in at the reception counter tucked beside the stairs.

She suppressed a shudder and went back outside, leaving the problematic front door still cracked open while she retrieved her sleeping bag and luggage from the car. With the exception of what she had deposited in the bank, all her worldly possessions were now able to be carried in two over-burdened trips and set inside on the faintly-patterned carpet in the parlor.

Coffee, she thought. *I need coffee and lanterns. Or a stiff drink.*

She pulled her coat out of the backseat, buttoned it tightly against the creeping chill, and quickly drove down the hill the three blocks over to the main street, looking around her as she went in an attempt to remember the route to take back to her new home. The Inn had been built on the top of a scenic bluff overlooking the sprawling little town and the wide beach and ocean just beyond it. The streets were often curved to match the topography as they dropped toward sea level, and were clean and quiet. Rows of small shops with lit window displays lined the sidewalks, and antique-style street lamps were just flickering on in the semi-darkness.

Driving on Main Street, it looked like the town had rolled up the sidewalks for the night right before she arrived. *Not exactly LA*, she thought, but then she hadn't actually loved Los Angeles. It had been where she lived and where she worked, but she'd never really felt at home there. This old beach town was as different from her last town as it could be, with charming little side streets full of well-kept bungalows and locally-owned small shops. She could just see an open town square that the people probably used as a park, with a painted white bandstand and benches scattered around the sidewalk-enclosed lawn. The main patio had a permanent stand in place for the town's annual Christmas tree and Amanda guessed that the stone monument nearby was probably for war veterans or to honor a local hero or city founder. The raw ocean air was almost tangy with salt.

No smog or hot pavement here, she thought, *but I'll probably miss Starbucks on every corner and going out for carb-free lunches.*

Amanda had seen a general store with a large sign that boasted "hardware" when she first drove into town, and she silently prayed that it would still be open this late. She parked in front of the old movie theater and had to jog the last few yards to catch the attention of the dark-haired store owner, who had a gray cat tucked under his arm and was just flipping over the CLOSED sign in the front window. He looked up in surprise but nodded and let her in under the green awning, setting the large cat on the floor as he pulled open the door. The cat strolled over to the main counter and hopped up, its yellow eyes soberly watching as Amanda hurried inside.

"Thank you so much for letting me in! I just need a couple of things and I'll be out of here before you know it. Do you have any lanterns?" She stopped to scratch the unenthusiastic cat under the chin, and followed the store owner down an aisle packed with crab traps and boxes of Mason jars. The whole store smelled of history; of fresh fruit and cardboard and smoked fish and motor oil, and decades of townspeople and visitors who had stopped by to get supplies or ask advice.

Just past the old-fashioned woodstove and some well-worn benches clustered around it, her host stopped in front of a display of lanterns.

"Oil or battery?" he asked.

"Battery," she said. "Don't want to burn the place down my first night there." Amanda flashed back to her friend's recommendation to just torch the place so she could sell a vacant lot, and she suppressed a grin.

The clerk cocked an eyebrow in surprise as he pulled a box down from the top shelf. "This one won't burn down anything. Um, first night where?"

Amanda mentally winced. "The Ravenwood Inn. I inherited it from my aunt and uncle and just came into town. Figured I'd stay there tonight and get a better look at things in the morning."

He gave a low whistle. "Lady, you've got guts. That place needs some serious help." He looked her over, not trying to disguise it. "So you're Conrad and Judy's niece, huh? You going to just live at the Inn or open it as a bed and breakfast again?"

"Both."

He grinned and stuck out a large hand. "I think you're going to be a very good customer of mine. My name's Brian Petrie and I'm the owner here. If you need anything, let me know."

She shook his hand, laughing. "I'm Amanda Graham. I'm afraid I might be *too* good of a customer. The Inn needs a lot of work to get back in shape. You don't happen to have a frequent buyer discount, do you?"

"For people who fix up historic old buildings that are probably full of spiders and ghosts? I'm sure we can figure something out." His smile was warm, and for the first time since she'd come to Ravenwood Cove, Amanda started to relax a bit.

"Just don't mention spiders, okay? I'm sleeping on the floor. Got any cots for sale? And bug spray?"

***

By the time Amanda walked out of the hardware store her arms were full of packages and bags. She waved clumsily at Brian, watching him flip over the CLOSED sign again, and stuffed her loot into her small car. It took a bit of maneuvering to push her purchases aside enough to wedge behind the wheel and close the door.

Gonna need a larger car for the Inn, she mused. *Something I can use to pick up people and groceries, and transport building supplies.* Pulling away from the curb, her thoughts were full of the future business, with images of lots of happy tourists booking reservations to stay at her beautiful historic inn and Amanda as their smiling, always welcoming hostess.

It was just the sort of dream that she really wanted to make come true.

She wasn't afraid of hard work. Her last job had been as a fraud investigator for a large insurance company, and she had practically run the team. Her boss had been a well-meaning alcoholic with a habit of disappearing shortly after lunch and then coming in the next day with a colossal hangover. Amanda had taught herself a lot of the investigation techniques, learning how to tell when someone was lying to her to get a chunk of settlement money, or when a restaurant's devastating fire was really a case of arson to pay off the owner's debts. She'd seen more than her share of how greedy and manipulative other humans could be. Between that and an ex-boyfriend who never missed an opportunity to let her know if she'd gained a few pounds or which girls at a party were prettier than her, she was tired right down to her soul.

A new career and a huge project like the Inn was exactly what she needed. No men, no drama.

Thank goodness small towns didn't have any secrets or excitement.

Chapter 2

Amanda awoke the next morning to the harsh sound of an enthusiastically-crowing rooster somewhere down the street. Bright sunshine streamed through the small cracks in the boards that were nailed over the dirty windows on the ground floor. A quick jump out of her cot and a lot of frantic checking of her bedding later, she was able to give a deep sigh of relief.

No spiders! That was definitely a good start to the day. Checking the clock on her phone, she cursed softly. It was much earlier than she normally got up, and certainly a crowing rooster was entirely different than the normal traffic sounds she was used to outside her condo window in LA.

Damn chicken.

She tied her long hair back into a scruffy ponytail and grabbed her flashlight, then began a methodical survey of the Inn, jotting quick notes in her notebook about the floor plan and taking photos of the condition of each room. The main floor had a formal dining room next to a huge, if a bit old-fashioned, professional kitchen. A dark wood door led to a large tiled powder room, complete with a huge, extravagantly-framed mirror. Two oversized parlors were obviously the main areas to entertain; one with an attached sunroom and a sheet-draped piano and the other boasting an enormous fireplace, complete with an iron swing arm to hang a kettle on. There was a full laundry tucked just off the kitchen, and another door toward the back. She opened it, shining her flashlight downward. A painted

15

wooden staircase led downstairs to a dark basement, and she caught a whiff of cold brick and old dirt. Amanda shuddered and closed the door. Definitely something she'd check out after the lights came back on.

Closing the cellar door she turned and started walking up the stairs next to it, emerging on the next floor at the end of a wide hallway. *Servant stairs,* she thought to herself, realizing that this route was for easy access, not broad and designed to impress like the main staircase. Going upstairs she discovered six large bedrooms; three that had their own bathrooms and a view of the distance beach, and all with small balconies. The furniture looked old, but sturdy and in good shape. She pulled open the heavy drapes carefully, welcoming the sunlight brightening the rooms even as she held her breath against the sudden cloud of dust.

Unlatching the French doors on one of the balconies overlooking the derelict orchard, she swung them wide and took in a deep breath. There were so many fruit trees outside that she could actually catch the scent of ripe apples on the morning breeze. She hadn't realized that several acres of land came with the Inn, along with a few sturdy outbuildings. A large rose-covered pergola was right next to the path leading into the orchard, and a couple of sheds, a small stable, and lone chicken coop were set at the very back of the property.

Closer to the Inn a tangled mess of weeds and a forlorn, leaning scarecrow marked what had previously been at least half an acre of garden, surrounded by a short picket fence. She knew that the Ravenwood used to provide meals for guests, and wished she'd asked her uncle more questions about the day-to-day life of running a historic bed and breakfast. Perhaps some cook long ago had been able to rush outside to get the fresh herbs or extra tomatoes they needed for dinner, or bring back fresh eggs for breakfast.

Maybe Amanda could even get some chickens. She chuckled, picturing herself chasing squawking hens around while searching for eggs. She definitely was *not* a country girl.

She took the main stairway up another floor and found two small bedrooms, probably for servants, and a large suite that was obviously the owners' living quarters. Every room she had discovered still had the original furniture there, covered in dust and sometimes cobwebs, but the owners' room was the first where it was in chaos. Unlike the other neatly-arranged bedrooms, this one had clothes strewn on the floor and every drawer in the dresser pulled wide open. The bed was unmade, with blankets dumped onto the floor and papers still scattered wildly across the desktop.

She'd known that her aunt and uncle left suddenly years before, but this had all the signs of someone fleeing in a hurried panic. When she'd visited her uncle in Kansas he had told her they hadn't lived in Ravenwood for years, but never offered the reason for their move, or why they'd left a thriving business behind.

Amanda was careful, walking over the strewn clothes and discarded papers and trying not to step on anything. How many years had this poor place been left to rot? Why would her uncle and aunt suddenly flee, with so many personal possessions and expensive furniture still here? *People leave when they're afraid,* she thought, picking up an overturned chair and setting it on its legs. *They run away when they're being chased and don't want to get caught.*

Amanda had already felt like she was a visitor as she walked through room after room that looked as if they just needed to be cleaned up to be ready to greet guests again, but seeing the suite where her uncle and aunt had lived and then suddenly left, Amanda felt almost like she was trespassing in someone else's private life. It seemed like just another reminder that she didn't really know much about her last relatives' lives, and since she was now by herself, that opportunity had passed her by.

She backed out quietly and shut the door. It'd be best to sleep in one of the other rooms before she'd try tackling cleaning out the mess and the history in that one. Too many secrets in there.

After a quick breakfast of cheese and crackers, she was ready to start. She made a few calls to set up an account with the local electric company, to order a subscription to the local paper and delivery of a dumpster for remodeling debris, and to check with the local assessor about any back taxes. Uncle Conrad had mentioned once, years ago, that paying the taxes on the Inn was killing him, but that he wasn't ready to stop yet. Whatever kept him writing out yearly checks to Ravenwood Cove for an inn that he didn't live in anymore was a boon to Amanda, since it had no liens on it and it hadn't been sold at auction.

With no past debts to worry about and the promise of electricity by noon, she grabbed a crowbar and some work gloves and headed outside. By the time she had pried the second board off, she could feel that someone by the street was watching her.

Let them gawk, she thought. *Not like they've never seen a woman doing remodeling before, was it?*

"Good morning!" The voice was authoritative, masculine, and definitely meant to get her attention.

She turned around, still clutching the bleached piece of lumber she'd just wrestled off the window, and wished she had a free hand to brush her hair away from her face. The middle-aged police officer standing behind her was smiling but it didn't go up to his eyes. His facial expression was all business.

"I don't believe we've met." It was a statement that expected an answer.

Amanda set the board down, annoyed at the interruption, and pulled off her work glove. "I'm Amanda Graham, the new owner of the Ravenwood Inn. My uncle left it to me and I'm fixing it up a bit."

He shook her hand, gripping it firmly, and gave her a genuine smile. "I'm George Ortiz, the police chief for Ravenwood Cove. Welcome to our little village. You're pretty good with that crowbar."

Surprised, Amanda laughed. "Thanks. It's my first time."

George's eyes roamed over the peeling paint and warped floorboards of the front porch. "I wish you luck with your project. I've always wanted to see inside this old place but it's been abandoned so long I haven't had a chance. Do you think I could get a tour sometime?"

"How about now?" She smiled, laying the board and crowbar on the decking and cleaning her hands off as she straightened up. It wouldn't hurt to take a break, and she certainly wasn't going to start off on the wrong foot with the local police.

She took George through the entire Inn with a feeling of pride at the potential that she was showing him, and he nodded whenever she told him about her plans for a certain room or possibilities for what she could do at the Inn in the future. The police chief was full of ideas and comments when she told him her ideas for the various rooms, and she took notes on which contractors and tradespeople he recommended. By the time they'd reached the third floor she'd learned not to hire the Hortman brothers as her plumbers, because they drank on the job, and that contractor Roy Greeley gave the best job for the best price, as long as she didn't have him do any electrical work because he'd nearly burnt down his own shed.

Life in a small beach town, she thought. *Of course the police chief knows everyone.*

"I'll send the Reverend by later today. Looks like you could use some serious help with the grounds."

Amanda peeked around him, through the smudged window to the back part of the property. Fallen tree limbs and decaying piles of leaves were tangled in the knee-high weeds. "The church does yard care? Or do you think I just need prayer to get this place back in shape?"

George laughed. "Not exactly. They have a youth group that raises money for charity and the Reverend makes sure they do a good job for a good price. My wife and I hire them to mow our yard every week, and it helps keep the teenagers busy and outta trouble."

When Amanda opened the door to the owners' suite, showing the scattered mess inside, George gave a low whistle.

"Maid's day off?"

She shrugged, unapologetic. "Was this way when I did the walkthrough, and I just haven't had a chance to clean it up yet."

"Looks like someone left in a hurry." The police chief stepped carefully into the room, his eyes sweeping over the chaos.

Amanda nodded, suddenly feeling protective of the mess, although she didn't exactly know why. "My uncle and aunt left really suddenly one day, and they never talked about it. I think they hired someone from town to board up the windows. I don't know if they ever came back to visit."

George corrected her. "The city council paid for the windows downstairs to be boarded up because they were worried about kids breaking them for fun or getting inside and making mischief. The Inn is the oldest structure in town, and one of the most historic." He walked through the room, looking at everything but not touching, and Amanda had the sudden sensation that that was exactly what he did at a crime scene.

"They never told you why they left in such a rush?"

Amanda shook her head. "I don't think they told anyone. When I tried to ask once, Uncle Conrad just said it was in the past, and to leave it there."

George flipped over an open book with his foot. "By the way, you're going to have to talk to the city council about your plans for the Inn, being it's on the historic rolls and all. You're not going to paint this place purple or turn it into a meditation center or something like that, are you?"

Amanda laughed as she ushered him out the bedroom door and back into the hallway. "Not hardly. I want the Inn to be what it was in the past. Elegant and beautiful." She thought for a moment, and added, "Hopefully loved, too."

"Well, I hope you can make a go of it." He shook her hand again when he left, and though his words sounded positive, there was a faint tone of doubt in his voice.

Fine, she thought. *Another person who thinks I can't make this business work.*

She was discovering that nothing motivated her as much as someone saying no, or telling her she couldn't accomplish something. Maybe it was her stubborn nature, or maybe it was because of all the times someone had disappointed her, but it seemed like other people's opinions meant less and less to her as she moved toward what she needed in her life.

After George left, Amanda got her crowbar and started working again on the boarded up windows. By noon she had almost all of the ground floor free of lumber, and light was streaming in through the smeared glass. It was as if the old building, shuttered for so long, was emerging from its frozen slumber, and Amanda was the one magically awakening it.

Chapter 3

As the day wore on, it was readily apparent that she was drawing a crowd. There was a steady parade of people quietly strolling by the front of her property, openly staring at what was happening to the long-abandoned Inn. Several people had come forward to introduce themselves as the local electrician, plumber, or painter, and she politely took their cards and answered their endless questions about her plans for the Ravenwood. She could tell some people wanted her business, and some just wanted to be able to tell their friends the latest gossip about the strange woman with the crowbar down at the Inn.

By the time she'd met the cheerful local reporter, Lisa Wilkins, and had posed for a quick photo on the wide front porch, she was wishing that she'd been more careful with her hair and makeup, and realizing that she wasn't just a new resident. She was a new event in the small town, like some circus or traveling art show. It was definitely out of her comfort zone.

Eventually she found a broom in the utility room, and started sweeping the dead leaves and dirt off the front porch. Within minutes she could see that her neighbors who lived across the street were solemnly filing out of their garage, each family member carrying a folding chair. The parents chose a spot on their lawn, facing across the road toward the front part of the Inn, and pointed to where the three kids could set up their own chairs. Amanda was trying to keep her head tucked down so they couldn't see her sneaking surreptitious glances their way, but once the family had brought out a lunch basket and were making sandwiches and drinking soda while they openly watched her, she couldn't help but stifle a giggle.

Nothing good on TV, she thought. *I must be way more entertaining, I guess. Might as well grab this bull by the horns.*

She straightened up, smiling broadly and waving at her audience, until finally the mother waved back, still clutching her sandwich.

Amanda put down her broom and was just about to walk over and introduce herself, when a large tan van pulling a small trailer drove up next to her brick mailbox. She walked close and as soon as the van was stopped in her circular drive, about a half dozen teenagers spilled out. The driver was last, walking around the car, his pleasant face wreathed in smiles as he stuck out his hand.

Amanda saw the cross painted on the side of the van, along with the words Ravenwood Cove Presbyterian Church. "You must be the Reverend." She shook his hand, watching the teens leaning against the side of the car. "And this must be the work crew."

There was something warm and welcoming in the laugh lines around his eyes, and the openness of his face. "Yes, Mrs. Graham. I'm Thomas Fox. We thought we'd stop by and donate an afternoon's worth of work to your cause. Then, if we do a good job, maybe we can bid for your business."

Amanda corrected him about the Mrs. comment and showed them where to get started, in the front by the road. Once she was satisfied that they were going to spruce up the front flower beds and edge the lawn to her wishes, she went inside to get the kitchen in shape enough that she'd at least be able to store her food in there.

Fearing the worst, she took a big gulp of fresh air and whipped open the refrigerator door. She had no idea how long the Inn had been without electricity. To her surprise it was empty and clean inside, as was the separate industrial-sized freezer. She checked through the tall cupboards, throwing out all the old boxes of food in a couple big plastic garbage cans from the utility room, and clearing away a clean space for her own groceries.

After letting the water in the main faucet run for a few minutes, she was relieved to discover it had transformed from a brownish-red to clear, letting her know that at least the pipes in the old building weren't going to be a problem for her. She had enough to deal with between the layers of dust and the family of mice she had found living behind the kitchen garbage can.

Buy bleach and paper towels. Red wine. Hire exterminator, she added to her list. Maybe she could find one that was humane.

By the end of her first day she had bought some groceries and cleaning supplies, met her spectator family from across the street, the Hendersons, and fed cookies and sodas to the entire church work crew. She'd also killed four spiders, gotten electricity and light in the Inn to chase away the ghosts lingering in the shadows, and hired an inspector and contractor to see what needed to be done. She'd scrubbed, swept, carried and chatted until every muscle in her entire body screamed in protest.

I won't need a gym membership, she thought as she shuffled into the relatively clean guest room she'd previously chosen on the second floor and dropped on the freshly-made bed in utter exhaustion. *If this Inn doesn't whip me into shape, nothing will.*

She was asleep within minutes, dreaming of dancing ghosts of the past waltzing in the foyer, and fat mice in the kitchen.

Chapter 4

By the afternoon of the third day she could see real progress. It felt good to pull the tangled vines away from the foundation, and to supervise the yard crew. The teens had been put to work digging deeply into the rich dirt of the garden, hacking out the tree roots that had grown into it during the years it had lain fallow. They were doing a terrific job with the tough labor, laughing and joking in-between taking turns on the shovels, and Amanda was truly happy that she'd hired them.

The morning hadn't started out quite so well. Her local rooster had upped the ante by crowing at the crack of dawn right underneath her windowsill, and then streaking away in terror when Amanda had hoisted the sash and hurled a pillow at him. She'd muttered a few words that would've made her mother give her a stern lecture of disapproval, but it was worth it. He may have been a big, beautiful fellow with gorgeous tail feathers the colors of fall, but if he kept it up she was going to start researching recipes for chicken and dumplings.

The surly building inspector had come and gone, snooping in every corner of the building for over two hours, and pursing his lips while he made grunting sounds of disapproval. The extensive report he left behind actually wasn't as bad as Amanda had feared. The good news was that the Inn was basically sound, and no issues were found with the foundation, plumbing, or wiring. The bad news was that it desperately needed a new furnace, the windows would all have to be replaced due to crumbling sills, and a long-term roof leak at the back of the building had rotted out a huge chunk of the sunroom wall. The inspector had handed Amanda the printed report with the deadpan comment, "Coulda been much worse."

Roy Greeley, the contractor, was a wonder, and Amanda made a mental note to thank the police chief for his recommendation. Roy had brought his own small team of workers with him to start repairs right away, and after watching for a bit to make sure they knew what they were doing, Amanda was satisfied with their progress enough to head into the kitchen for some coffee, and to call to order the new double-paned windows. She had gulped when the guy on the phone told her the total cost, but pulled her credit card out of her wallet and glumly gave the salesclerk the numbers. It was nearly a third of the money she'd set aside for the total remodel, and she realized she'd have to find new ways to squeeze her budget. At this rate her funds would be gone far too soon, and she knew she couldn't open for paying guests until the work was completed. It was definitely going to be a race to see if her money ran out before she could get paying customers.

It was two o'clock before Amanda got a chance to sit down. With the high school group and Roy's crew taking a much-deserved lunch break, she could relax a bit herself. The crisp fall air carried the smoky scent of burning leaves, and she could see a drift of white smoke from somewhere down the road where one of her neighbors was probably burning yard debris. She retrieved her copy of the Ravenwood Tide, the local newspaper, off the front porch and settled into a wicker chair to read about the goings on in her new town.

The paper's front page had Amanda's picture on it. Her smile looked a bit nervous in the photo, but the article was accurate and to the point. It listed some of the work that was expected to be done on the Inn, and Amanda's new ownership after her aunt and uncle had left town eight years before. Lisa, the reporter, had made sure her quotes were exact, putting in Amanda's comments about the remodel and her hopes for having the Inn open for guests soon.

She gets points for not using the word 'abandoned', Amanda thought, and turned the page.

The rest of the paper was a slice of life from her new hometown. Kazoodles Toy Store was having a sidewalk sale, weather permitting. The volunteer fire department was hosting a pancake breakfast at the Grange hall to raise money for much-needed equipment. Mrs. Welch was missing her diamond necklace and offering a reward. This month was the best time to plant garlic and start a new compost pile.

Not exactly LA, Amanda mused, folding the paper. *Maybe the article about the Inn will bring some new business my way.*

With that happy thought, she grabbed a hammer and a box of nails so she could tack down some loose boards on the small porch by the back door. It was separate from the main front porches, just off the kitchen. Definitely not as elegant as the sunroom on the other end of the house, it probably had been a welcome resting spot for kitchen staff who'd been on their feet too much in a hot kitchen while cooking for a houseful of guests, or for servants needing a break from people wanting their time and attention.

Amanda was almost ready to pound the first nail into a floorboard when she caught a rustle of movement out of the corner of her eye. She turned her head just in time to see a plump woman with a Russian-style headscarf tied under her chin. The woman was gaping at Amanda, standing under one of the laden apple trees and holding a split-wood basket over one arm, her practical shoes deep in the fallen fruit on the ground.

Amanda straightened up and smiled, but her mysterious visitor turned and ran like a woman possessed, not minding the fruit bouncing out of her basket as she fled. She quickly pushed one of the tall fence boards aside and slipped through the gap, into the yard of a small bungalow next door.

That's it, Amanda thought, irritated. *My neighbors are flat out weird.*

She didn't mind sharing the bushels of apples that were being neglected in her orchard and she certainly didn't mind a visitor, but she was going to have to get used to people thinking her life, and apparently her land, was open for public use and scrutiny.

***

A couple of hours later and the contractor crew and the teenage workers were back at their jobs. Amanda was scraping the paint from a carved wooden porch railing on the side of the Inn when her contractor walked up to her. Roy was accompanied by a tall, elegant woman and from the look on his face Amanda could tell he was none too pleased about it.

"Amanda, I've brought someone here to meet you. This is Mrs. Sandford, Ravenwood Cove's mayor."

31

Amanda smiled warmly, but the glacial expression on the older woman's face remained unchanged. She looked Amanda over carefully, as if she were a specimen in a zoo. An ugly specimen.

One that she wants to eat, Amanda thought.

"The mayor's come to see the progress on the Inn." Amanda could hear the faint note of warning in Roy's voice, and from his tone and the mayor's rigid posture, she could tell something was definitely wrong.

She restrained the impulse to curtsey to the tall, somber woman and instead shook the mayor's cool hand.

"It's a pleasure to meet you, Mayor Sandford. I was going to come by to check about what I needed to do to satisfy the historical society on restoring the Inn. Don't want to get off on the wrong foot with the town, do I?"

The mayor sniffed and looked pointedly at the long peels of old paint that clung to the front porch. "I do hope you're considering this as a dwelling and not a business, Miss Graham. With the exception of month-long or more rentals, Ravenwood Cove does not allow short term occupation."

Amanda was stunned, and her face showed it. "Um, I'm sorry, but I don't understand. You mean you don't allow bed and breakfasts, or hotels? In a beach town?"

Mrs. Sandford inclined her head gravely at Amanda. "Ravenwood Cove has never been some wild tourist hot spot, Miss Graham. I hope you understand that our residents prefer a more sedate, quiet type of living here. They're used to having all the benefits of living in a beautiful and secure coastal town, without the horrid traffic and litter and problems that a tourist-driven economy would incur."

"Wait! You mean that the local merchants don't want tourists and families to visit here, too? Have you asked them?"

The mayor gestured to the workers installing new floorboards on the porch, and digging the weeds out of the garden. "I commend you for being so meticulous in the upkeep of your home, but I can tell you now that the city council would not be able to approve such a drastic step as to convert this structure to a hotel."

Amanda could feel her blood pressure shoot up as she listened to the pompous words of the imperious woman in front of her. "This structure?" She gestured widely toward the Inn, her sole source of future income and the only thing of value she owned except for her car. "This place has been hosting guests for decades! There wouldn't be any conversion, because it's always been a hotel. God only knows how many people have visited here! Mr. Petrie told me that the Inn is the oldest building in town."

Mrs. Sandford ran a languid hand up the nearby column, cracking off paint chips under her blue-veined fingers. "Maybe the oldest, but that doesn't mean it needs to be back in business." She wiped her hands together briskly, as though signaling the end of the conversation. "We have to protect the town against an influx of tourists and the problems that riff-raff who don't belong in the town bring with them. I'm sure you understand. Besides, the neighborhood here is now residential." The mayor gestured down the quiet, cottage-lined street.

"This town grew up around the Ravenwood Inn, and surely its original function is grandfathered in, isn't it? Just like farms that have towns build up around them and they get to keep their livestock. Should be the same thing. What do you mean it's now residential?"

"I'm sorry, but no. Since this structure was abandoned so long, I believe the zoning has been changed to fit the new type of neighborhood."

Amanda could feel the pressure between her ears, and her hands were actually shaking. "Do you know this means I'll be completely broke? I've been putting every dime I have into fixing this place up. I can't afford to even *live* in the Inn, if it isn't bringing in any money."

Mrs. Sandford looked at her with rock-hard eyes. "It is regrettable, but the town must be protected. You are welcome to bring your concerns before the town council, of course."

Amanda tried to keep her voice calm. "And are you on the town council, Mayor?"

For the first time, her guest's mouth flexed in a semblance of a smile. "Of course. As mayor, I head the council."

Amanda's mind scrambled wildly, trying to come up with things to say that would possibly sway the imperious old bat.

"We believe in preserving the tranquility of the town at all costs, Miss Graham."

"Even at the expense of your residents? I'm a resident, too, Mayoir Sandford!"

The frosty smile faded from the mayor's thin lips. "Miss Graham, my family has been here for generations. Many of the best buildings in town were originally built and owned by my relatives. Your family stayed here just long enough to leave in the dead of night years ago, under very odd circumstances." She sniffed. "Not exactly a solid family legacy."

For the first time in memory, Amanda couldn't think of anything to say, at least anything that didn't have four letters in it.

Apparently Mrs. Sandford could detect the rising rage that Amanda was trying to control. "Hmmmm. How unfortunate that unwholesome tempers run in your family. I'm afraid that I must be going. Good day, Miss Graham."

As the tall mayor turned to go, ignoring Amanda's stunned look, there was a scuffle of commotion in the garden, and a chorus of sharp exclamations. Amanda turned to see what had happened, just as one of the tallest teenage boys ran over to her.

"Um, Miss Graham?" Amanda could see the desperation on the boy's face.

"Yes?"

"I think we just found a dead body in your garden."

Chapter 5

Nightmare. This had to be a nightmare, because surely her life couldn't get any worse.

The tall boy was right. There was definitely something buried under the scarecrow.

Only it wasn't a something. It was a someone.

One of the workers had been digging out tree roots about three feet down when he'd caught a glimpse of something unusual in the bottom of the hole. His spade had pulled away enough dirt from the clear plastic that Amanda could make out the skeletal outline of a human hand, and a glimpse of a dark piece of fabric, maybe a sleeve.

Several people already had their cell phones out to call the police, and Amanda could only imagine how busy the small town's emergency dispatcher was going to be.

The next few hours were a blur of unwanted, horrible activity. The entire parking area for the Inn was taken up by police cars and townspeople who had driven over so they could see the excitement up close and personal. Roy stayed with Amanda on the side porch, explaining who was who, and bringing her a steaming mug of coffee as the evening's chill set in. The police chief had arrived first, and had asked the stunned owner of the Ravenwood Inn to sit in one spot, in case he had any questions.

"No media vans? I'm surprised."

Roy shrugged. "Too far from the big guys to drive over. Probably get a lone reporter with a camera guy here in the next day or so."

Pretty certain this isn't the tranquility the mayor had been talking about, she thought, as she watched a young police officer unroll yellow crime scene tape and tie it to the bare lilac bushes at the edge of the road. Mrs. Sandford had stayed for just fifteen minutes, frantically talking at breakneck speed into her cell phone while the entire contingent of local emergency responders, including paramedics and volunteer firefighters, showed up to witness the excitement happening at Amanda's historic Inn.

"I'm thinking those paramedics are too late," she commented to Roy as the ambulance crew pulled out a gurney and sat on it, watching the people milling around the garden. "The poor guy is dead, after all."

Roy's face was deadpan. "You've got a weird sense of humor, Amanda."

She shrugged. "Seems appropriate today."

Roy took a sip of his cooling coffee. "Just a slow day for them. You have to understand that not much happens around here, and they want to check out the action." Roy waved a paint-spattered hand at the neighbors across the street, openly sitting outside and watching the crowd accumulate. "This is big stuff in a small town like Ravenwood Cove."

A white minivan pulled in to the circular front drive and drove up the edge of the tape, waiting as a young police officer hurried to move it aside so the van could drive through.

"Who's that?"

"That's Ben, the mortician. Guess the medical examiners was unavailable so Ben's going to transport the remains. The funeral home doesn't use hearses anymore except for funerals. Ben says that way they don't creep people out when they're driving dead people around, and no one messes with their cars."

Amanda suppressed a shiver. Dead bodies. Who'd want to mess with that?

The contractor chuckled. "Can you imagine someone carjacking that minivan when someone's lying in the back? That'd be a surprise for them."

"You've got a sick sense of humor, too, Roy."

Roy sighed deeply. "Yeah, that's what my wife tells me."

She should've expected it, but when the police chief came over with a warrant to search the Inn, specifically the main suite, Amanda's heart flipped over in her chest. Her hands were trembling when she held the piece of paper, reading the details. George sounded a bit apologetic when he explained that his team would need full access to the Inn, that she was allowed to stay in one room while they searched, and that they'd do their best not to damage anything.

It was official. Her family and her Inn were the first suspects.

It took hours for the police to process the crime scene, and to remove the adult-sized skeletal remains from Amanda's garden. The tall spotlights they'd brought in still illuminated the trampled backyard, now littered with tarps and tape. They'd also photographed every square inch of the disheveled master suite, and carried out several brown paper bags full of evidence.

By the time the police chief came over to where she was sitting on the porch, it was nearly midnight. Wrapped in a heavy quilt, the night air was cold on Amanda's face, and she could see fatigue in every line of George's body as he dropped gratefully into an open chair.

"I know you've got a lot of questions, Amanda."

She snorted. "You *think*? Do you have any idea who that guy is...was?"

George ran his hand over the back of his neck, stretching his sore back at the same time. "Well, the official word won't be back from the lab for a while, but I'm pretty sure I know who it is."

Amanda leaned over, breathless.

"I think it's Emmett Johnson. He always wore this signet ring on his right pinkie finger, and it looked to me like it was the exact same one we just dug up."

Amanda's mind was reeling. Emmett Johnson. Someone who was known in this town, and had been buried in her backyard. Even though she'd never heard of him before, she knew she'd never forget his name.

Emmett.

"Are you sure?"

"I'd bet good money on it. Emmet used to wear a pair of ostrich-skin cowboy boots all the time. Looks like the fancy steel toe tips are right around where his feet are...were."

"Well, if it is Emmett, how long's he been in my garden?"

Amanda could see the hesitation on the police chief's face.

"Emmett's been missing for eight years."

Her mouth fell open. "You mean he –"

"Disappeared the same day your aunt and uncle left town, Halloween night over eight years ago." The police chief turned, and she caught a look of near-pity on his face.

"Right after your uncle told him to go to hell."

Chapter 6

Amanda didn't sleep much that night, and when she did her dreams were as tangled as the sweat-soaked sheets on her bed. Even when her boyfriend had left her she had endured the humiliation and pain without crying, but the last couple of days made her want to curl up in a ball and sob. Well, and maybe eat a half gallon of rocky road ice cream all by herself.

She felt defeated and tired down to the bottom of her soul. Losing her business, maybe losing her home, due to some stiff-necked locals and a corpse buried out back. It was just another disaster in the string of problems she'd had in her life, but she wasn't sure how she was going to get out of this one. She'd always been able to make plans on where she could land and what her next step would be, but a murder investigation and losing everything she owned definitely wasn't anything like her normal, small disasters.

She also kept thinking about the fact that maybe her family was the reason that guy had been buried out back. It'd be great if that wasn't a possibility, but the look in George's eyes said it was. Amanda kept thinking back to the police chief's words and what the look on his face implied.

Dead guy in the garden who disappeared same day he'd had an argument with her uncle. No wonder the cops had used a warrant to search the Inn.

She knew her Uncle Conrad wasn't a warm person or particularly friendly, but she couldn't picture him as a killer who'd literally plant the evidence right in his backyard.

It was true she hadn't really known her uncle or Aunt Judy well until her mother died two months before she was heading off for college. Amanda's father had left when she was two and for as long as she could remember her mom had been the only one who was always there for her. She'd never seemed very interested in keeping in touch with her brother-in-law and his wife, and brushed off Amanda's occasional questions about them as unimportant. Amanda's aunt and uncle may have meant well when they had her over for Thanksgiving dinner in their tiny apartment, but the truth was that they just didn't have much in common with a college student. They both seemed to be beaten down by their lives, and Uncle Conrad's face was always set in a mask of tired bitterness. They didn't seem to know how to relate to a younger generation at all, and her aunt had a hangdog appearance every time Amanda saw her, as if life was perpetually disappointing. Conversations were stilted or full of carefully-chosen neutral topics, while all the while Amanda was pushing the food around on her plate and counting the minutes until she could hug them goodbye and get out the door.

She couldn't say that she loved them, but she couldn't see them murdering anyone either, and from her brief conversation with the police chief, she was sure her uncle was on the short list of suspects.

All that time she'd know them, and maybe she hadn't really known them at all.

She was just pulling on a clean shirt and zipping up her jeans when she heard a loud knocking on the front door, downstairs. *More cops or journalists*, she thought. By the time she'd run down the stairs and yanked open the heavy door, she was out of breath, and looking up into the disapproving eyes of a tall man dressed in a dark brown bomber jacket and jeans.

"You always take this long to answer the door?"

She'd had it. After a nearly-sleepless night and a parade of rubber-necking townspeople, she was more than fed up with being polite and reasonable.

"You always this cranky before breakfast? Who the hell are you, anyway?"

He'd been looking over her head into the foyer behind her, but at the sharp tone of her voice his eyes snapped back to her face, and he pulled out a large police badge.

"I'm Detective James Landon of the county sheriff department. I've been assigned this case, and I came over to see what the local boys missed."

Amanda felt a surge of anger. She'd only been in town less than a week, but she already liked the local police she'd met.

"Well, prepare to be disappointed. They took just about everything out of my garden and the master suite, so I'm not sure what's left to see, if anything."

She pulled the door open and let the tall detective inside. He hung up his leather jacket on the hall tree and followed Amanda's retreating figure into the kitchen. He knew a woman who needed coffee when he saw one.

He was right. It took only a couple of minutes for her to fill the coffeemaker with water and shovel in some grounds. She pulled out two mugs and spoons, and gestured for him to sit at the long wooden table.

"I take it you're not here to talk to me about stranger danger or a neighbor complaint?"

He shrugged his broad shoulders and snorted in surprise. "You seem to be pretty nonchalant about what's going on. You always like this?"

Amanda pushed a stray strand of hair out of her eyes. "Yep. Every time they dig up somebody out of my yard, this is exactly what I do. Make coffee. Crack bad jokes." She sighed. "Look, I'm not exactly myself. Let's start over, okay?" She stuck out her hand. "I'm Amanda."

He shook her hand, grinning a bit. "I'm Detective Landon and I've been assigned to this case. Call me James."

"Deal. Want cream and sugar?"

By the time two steaming mugs of coffee were poured and doctored, James was listing what was going to happen with her case.

Her case. As if she had killed this guy herself.

"So the autopsy will tell us more, but it's been long enough that the coroner may not be able to determine a cause of death. We won't know for a bit. There's not a lot to...work with."

Amanda tried not to think about that. "Look, I hate to be practical, but I need to know what I can do and what I can't. The cops are saying that I can't work on some parts of my Inn until their investigation is over, and the mayor capped that off by saying that even if I do get this place up and running, she won't allow me to use it as a business." She looked across the table at the detective, his large hands wrapped around the warmth of the oversized coffee cup. "I'm getting tired of people telling me what I can't do, especially the mayor."

James shrugged. "Officially, I can only tell you about the police part but I grew up around here. My folks and my brothers are all still here, so I can tell you a thing or two about our esteemed mayor that would curl your toes."

He pulled a cookie off the plate that Amanda offered. "She likes to act like she's the queen, but she's got a past and issues just like everyone does. She just hopes no one remembers all of them."

"Okay, so what do you recommend? Blackmail? Voodoo doll?"

James shook his head. "Lawyer." From Amanda's facial expression, he could tell she didn't like that idea at all.

"And don't talk about blackmailing anyone, okay? I'd hate to have to come back here and slap some handcuffs on you."

She just caught the teasing gleam in his eye, even though his voice was steady and serious, and she broke out with a laugh.

"What if I rob a bank to pay for the lawyer?"

He took a big bite of his cookie, now openly grinning. "For that, lady, you get a free ride in a cop car and a one-way ticket to jail."

"Hey, at least it's free."

***

Amanda followed around after the detective, watching him take photos and scribble notes about various places in the Inn and outside in the yard. It was fascinating to see his keen mind trying to put together patterns and information out of seemingly random clues. She tried to keep quiet as she watched him work, but after over an hour of tagging along behind him, she was happy when they were both able to sit on the edge of the back porch and take a break.

"You know, Ravenwood Cove wasn't always like this, closed off to people. It was a great place to grow up. I bet I still know two-thirds of the people here."

Amanda thought of LA and the people she'd been around there. She didn't even know what her neighbor looked like, even though she'd lived next to him for a couple of years. She certainly didn't miss any of the people from her former workplace.

"You know anything about a really annoying rooster who likes to wake up the entire neighborhood at the crack of crack?"

The detective chuckled. "You mean Dumb Cluck? He's not gonna hurt you. He's just been around for years and thinks everything in the neighborhood belongs to him."

"He keeps waking me up this early I'm gonna put him in a crockpot."

James looked at her in mock disapproval. "Now, you don't want to do that. He's been here longer than you have. And also he'd be tougher to eat than an old boot."

"All right. He won't go in the crockpot, but how about I just duct tape his little beak shut?"

At his surprised look she raised her hands in surrender. "Just kidding!"

"Not much of a country girl, are you? Where are you from, anyway?"

"California." She swung her legs back in forth, enjoying the time off her feet.

He grunted. "Well, that explains it."

They sat in silence for a few minutes, just looking out at the backyard and the dug up garden.

James shifted gears a bit. "Tell me about your uncle. What sort of argument did he have with Emmett?"

"Look, I don't know anything about that. I only saw Uncle Conrad on holidays and he wasn't exactly the chatty sort. Also, are you sure this guy is Emmett? No one's told me officially yet."

James set his camera down on the wooden porch. "We won't know for sure until the dental records get confirmed, but it sure looks like it. Several people have verified the metal boot tips and ring found with the body."

"Did he have any family?"

James looked up, seemingly studying the passing clouds. "Not anyone who would claim him. You could say that he wasn't well-liked." He looked at her sideways. "By anyone."

"So there's no clue yet about how he died?"

James shook his head. "As soon as we know, I'll call you."

Amanda was surprised at the pang of disappointment she felt when he said that. *Would be nice to have him stop by instead*, she thought, looking over at the handsome lines of his face.

Get ahold of yourself. As she let him out the front door later, she mentally shook herself as she shut the door behind James' broad back. After everything she'd been through, the last thing she needed to be doing was speculating about whether her guest had been working out to get such broad shoulders, or if he was just naturally built like that.

She already had all the trouble she could handle, and eyeballing the local constabulary was just going to complicate her life further.

Now if she could only get her brain to obey that command, she'd be doing just fine.

Chapter 7

It wasn't easy being a small town celebrity.

Everywhere Amanda went, whether it was to stock up on groceries or to get her mail or to walk down to the beach for some quiet time, the silent eyes of the townspeople followed her. Most kept their distance, with maybe a small smile or quiet nod, but some stared outright or just ignored her as they walked by. At least her neighbors across the street had packed up the assortment of chairs they'd had on their front lawn to watch the parade of police, press, and officials that had come and gone once Emmett had been discovered.

Roy still showed up every day, without his crew, to lend a hand as he could. Some mornings he'd arrive a bit late, apologizing and explaining that he'd taken his boat out early to set a crab pot or two, and making sure to stay on Amanda's good side by dropping off a large Dungeness crab from time to time.

Amanda spent a lot of her frustration and anger on sanding the hardwood floors, stripping paint off the old shutters with a wire brush, and hoeing the weeds out of the curved flower borders near the front entrance. One day, while walking out to the mailbox she again caught a glimpse of her Slavic-looking neighbor at the bungalow next door. A pretty blonde woman was standing on the front porch, holding a big bag of groceries while the bundled-up lady gave her a hug and gestured for her to come inside. Amanda hadn't seen anyone over at the house since she'd seen the lady slip quickly through her fence to get out of the Inn's abandoned apple orchard, and the heavy curtains in her neighbor's windows were always closed.

Roy could see Amanda craning her neck a bit while she watched the neighbor go inside with her young visitor, and he had the answers all ready for the questions he knew Amanda would ask.

"That's Jennifer Peetman. She visits over there a couple o' times a week."

"Oh, really? Is she a relative?"

Roy wiped his dusty hands on his overalls. "Nah. She's just the only person around here who speaks any Russian, so she goes to take that lady stuff and visit with her. Just doing a good deed, I guess."

Amanda nodded. "Wish she'd tell her she could take all the apples she can carry. There's no way I'm going to use all the fruit I've got back there," she said, gesturing past the Inn.

Flipping open the local paper, Amanda scanned the front page. Not much more news about Emmett but they'd still made sure to take up as much space about it on the page as possible. Looks like the staff at the Ravenwood Tide was going to milk a rare crime story for everything they could. Compared to the announcements about Blackout Bingo Night to raise money for filling in potholes in front of the elementary school and that the local fisherman association was sponsoring an oyster-eating contest, the excitement of a murder won hands down.

As usual, Amanda ate her lunch outside on the front porch, taking a break from all the physical work and going over her list of things that still needed to be done. Sitting on the second step with her iced tea and tuna sandwich beside her, she was adding a few things to her shopping list when she heard an unfamiliar scratching sound.

She turned just in time to see a huge orange paw curl up from under the stairs and take a desperate swipe at her tuna sandwich, feeling around a bit on the plate as it tried to hook its long claws into Amanda's lunch.

"Hey!" she hollered and the paw jerked back, disappearing under the painted boards. Amanda was silent, straining to hear any sound from her unexpected and hungry guest, but heard nothing.

"Going to play hard to get, are ya?" she chuckled. Getting only silence in response, Amanda quietly gave her best cat-like meow. It had been years since she'd had a cat of her own, especially since Ken had been terribly allergic and hadn't liked cats. Any time she'd brought up the subject of getting a kitty, he'd look at her with his blond eyebrows raised in shock, as if she were an idiot, and change the subject.

She didn't miss Ken.

There was a pause, then a small meow back from under the broad steps. When Amanda tried again there was no answer, but she broke a corner off her sandwich, making sure there was plenty of fishy bits inside, and dropped it onto the grass at the side of the stairs. She leaned over, hoping that a free meal might tempt the would-be sandwich thief out into the sunshine, and after less than a minute the broad head of a striped orange cat emerged, glancing upward to watch Amanda with suspicion before taking the extra two steps to wolf down the tasty tidbit.

Amanda could see that the cat was lean, too lean, and that it had no collar. When she made little mewing sounds at it and then leaned over to try to pet it, the cat hissed softly at her, and quickly scrambled back to its hiding place.

"Have it your way, Mr. Kitty," she said, and pulled several more big chunks off her sandwich. She dropped them in the grass, close enough that the cat could smell them, and brushed the crumbs off her hands. "I wasn't that hungry anyway."

So much for making friends in Ravenwood, she thought. *Seems like I can't make friends with either people or animals.*

***

With the rest of the crew starting up their afternoon tasks, Amanda was free to head to town for a little research. The mayor had mentioned zoning, and when Amanda had talked to the city assessor about property taxes the first day she'd started to work on the Inn, he hadn't mentioned anything about a zoning issue.

It didn't take long to drive to City hall or to request the file on her property, but when the apologetic clerk brought out the card file, she was stilled stunned by what she saw. There, in black in white, was a newly-filed rezoning order, revoking any previous variance that had been in place. The taxable amount had been left the same, but the Ravenwood Inn, proud host to countless guests over decades of hospitality, was now just a single family home.

At the bottom of the card was one signature. Mrs. Sandford, dated the day she'd first met Amanda, and the day that Emmett had been discovered, buried in her garden.

Chapter 8

Amanda settled into the plush seat offered, and clutched her leather handbag on her lap.

"Thank you for seeing me on such short notice, Mr. Timmins."

The lean lawyer smiled at her from across his expansive antique desk. "Please, call me Charles. After your phone call it was apparent that you needed to talk to someone right away, and I'm happy to help."

"I just need some advice, and to figure out what I can and can't do, legally. I'm not sure where to start and you're the only lawyer in town."

Charles chuckled. "Well, there are some benefits to being the only one. I've been able to help the families of Ravenwood Cove for over twenty years.   I write wills for people or contest fence lines or answer legal questions. I even got to help George Ortiz adopt his youngest daughter. Being a small town lawyer means I get to help solve my neighbors' problems, and maybe I can do the same thing for you." He rested the elbows of his linen blazer on the desktop and steepled his fingers. "You want to know if your Uncle Conrad killed Emmett Johnson."

There it was.

She took a deep breath. "That's exactly what I want to know. I also want to know what I can do for my business. This whole thing has tied up my project of getting the Ravenwood Inn up and running again. It's not that I'm unsympathetic to the fact that someone has died, but I have to be practical." She shifted a bit in her seat, embarrassed. "Sympathy doesn't pay the bills."

The lawyer's face seemed to reflect his concern. "Sounds like you have a lot at stake, Miss Graham. I can only tell you what I know, and what everyone else knew. Emmett was obsessed with your aunt, and your uncle knew it. I've never seen a man so jealous." He leaned forward, his soft brown eyes full of compassion. "I know it's not what you probably want to hear, but your uncle had a terrible temper. He was known all through town as a hothead."

Amanda grimaced. "So I've heard," she admitted. "Charles, do you know anything about the day my uncle and aunt left, or the day before?"

"I'm afraid I can't help you much with that, Miss Graham. I was out of town that week at a legal conference and only heard about it when I got back. All I know is that your uncle was heard yelling at Emmett in Ivy's Café, and told him to go to hell. The waitress told me all about it when I came in the next week."

"Serves town gossip with her coffee?" The thought of someone spreading tales about her family, whether it had been true or not, made the pit of Amanda's stomach hurt.

Charles' voice was soothing as he stood up to walk around the desk and sit in the large chair next to her. "It wasn't like that at all. When something happens in public, people are going to talk about it in public. There must've been fifteen people in that diner when the argument occurred." He took a deep breath.

55

"And there's more. If it proved that your uncle is the murderer, the surviving members of his family can file a civil lawsuit to sue the estate of your uncle." He watched Amanda's face carefully and continued. "That means they can go after whatever property that was his at the time of his death. And that includes the Ravenwood Inn."

Amanda's heart stood still, time suspended in the office while the lawyer's words resounded again and again in her ears.

Includes the Ravenwood Inn.

All that work, all that hope, gone. Along with every last bit of money she had. Any hope she'd had of a future suddenly felt like a distant dream.

"I checked the zoning, Charles. The assessor's office shows that the mayor rezoned the Inn the day she met me, so now it's strictly residential." Her words were flat and emotionless.

"Are you sure?" At Amanda's resigned nod, Charles began to bristle.

"That's horrible. She may have the authority to do it but that doesn't give her the right. Maybe I can figure a way around it legally. If you're going to make that Inn back into a business it's got to have business zoning."

Amanda blinked back the tears threatening to gather behind her eyes, and Charles leaned over to pull some tissues out of a box on the desktop, handing them to Amanda.

"I'm sorry, Charles. I'm not usually this emotional but I think everything is catching up to me. The lack of sleep, the hard work, all the problems here in town."

The lawyer's voice was soothing. "I'm on your side, Amanda. You can always come talk to me about anything, even if it's just to let off some steam. Look, just send the documents you have about your uncle's last wishes and I'll see what I can do. As of today I am officially on retainer."

"I'm not sure how I'm going to be able to pay you, Charles."

He smiled warmly. "Got a dollar?" She was confused but he waited patiently while she dug into her purse and produced a single dollar bill. He took it and laid it on his desk.

"There. It's official. You've paid me a retainer and now I'm your advocate. Care for a mint?" He offered Amanda an open tin of peppermints, but she smiled and shook her head no, understanding that he was trying to give her a chance to calm down a bit. Charles popped one in his mouth, then set the tin down and stood up, digging into the top drawer of his tall file cabinet. After a few seconds of flipping through the folders, he pulled out a sheet of paper, looked it over carefully, and handed it to her.

"Here's a list of your rights while your property is under investigation. The main thing is to remember that you have a lawyer on your side, and that you don't let anyone search without a warrant."

"Too late," Amanda commented dryly, but Charles shook his head, obviously disagreeing.

"No, not too late. They may be back later with other requests to search the Inn. Just always ask to see their ID and their paperwork and call me if you have any questions, okay? It'll also help if you send over copies of any legal papers you have about the Inn. I don't want you to have to handle this all alone. Murder investigations can be grueling, especially for the families involved."

Amanda's mind flashed back to the early morning visit from James Landon, and how he hadn't had a warrant when he arrived. She quickly decided not to share that gaffe with Charles, but she certainly wasn't going to let a mistake like that happen again.

No matter how good the cop looked in new jeans and a bomber jacket.

Chapter 9

Amanda wearily pushed open the coffeehouse door, ignoring the cheerful jingle of the bell over her head. The small shop was empty of people, and she shuffled to the counter. She was slowly reading the chalkboard menu when a short woman with blonde curls and a bright smile came out of the back room, wiping her hands on her apron.

"Good morning! What can I get for you?"

"Got anything with booze in it?"

The girl eyeballed Amanda and drew the right conclusion instantly. "Rough day?"

A deep sigh. "The cops think they've identified the dead guy in my garden."

The barista's mouth formed a surprised O, then snapped shut. "Well, I don't have booze, but how about a mocha? I could make you a double."

Amanda nodded at the suggestion and plopped down bonelessly into one of the overstuffed armchairs. Through the smear of raindrops tracking across the window she could see the hill sloping downward toward the quiet town. It looked deceptively peaceful, as if everyone always got along and just brought each other cake and loaned out their lawn mowers to their neighbors and had charity spaghetti feeds, but Amanda was starting to see a much different side of this little village. It was full of real people, with real lives and real problems, failings, and secrets.

It also once housed a murderer.

And that murderer may still be here. They could even be as close her own family.

The blonde lady brought over a big mug of steaming coffee topped with whipped cream and a dusting of cocoa, and handed it to her. She sat down on the nearby sofa, expectant.

"Look, you don't have to talk if you don't want to, but I know I haven't seen you around here before, and it's not every day someone comes in and tells me there's a dead guy in their yard."

"Garden," Amanda corrected her. She sighed again, knowing that she'd just have to tell the whole story, and wishing she was back in Los Angeles.

"Sorry; garden." The blonde woman leaned forward, her blue eyes full of kindness. "Yeah, I read about the whole thing. My name's Meg. Is there anything I can do for you?"

This was unexpected, and Amanda looked at the young woman carefully, sizing her up. There was a kindness and intelligence in her face that appealed to her, and she could feel her body relaxing into the comfy chair as she took the first sip of her coffee.

She'd been wound tight as a spring since that night they'd discovered Emmett, and the lack of sleep was definitely taking its toll. Almost without meaning to, Amanda started telling Meg about the grim discovery at the Inn, the mortician and cops, and the mayor's comments. She could feel the pinpricks of tears at the edge of her eyes as she went over what had been said about her family's possible involvement. Watching for Meg's reaction, she only saw kindness in her eyes and decided to keep talking. By the time she'd spun out the whole sordid tale, her new friend was nodding sympathetically.

"How horrible. I'm so sorry."

"I don't know what to do next. I do feel sorry for the dead man, but if he's Emmett Johnson like they think he is, he's been buried under that scarecrow for years. How do I find out who did it, and how do I find out…"

She couldn't say the words.

"If your uncle did it?" Meg's voice was carefully neutral.

Amanda couldn't think of anything to say, but her new friend went on.

"Look, I know you don't know me, but this coffee shop has two rules: serve delicious stuff, and what happens at Cuppa stays at Cuppa." She got up and pulled two fat cinnamon rolls out of the glass display case, put each ofthem on a plate, and handed one to Amanda.

"On the house. Tory – that's the owner - probably should've named this place The Confessional, because we're used to people coming in and talking about all sorts of stuff and we always keep it to ourselves." She sat down and pulled a chunk off her cinnamon roll, obviously thinking.

Amanda stared into her mug. "It just seems like I can't get a break, and like everyone's in my business. I don't think I can take much more of this."

"Then don't."

Amanda looked up, to see Meg looking at her with a serious expression on her face. "Don't take it anymore," she said. "You've got rights just like everyone else, and you live in this town, too. Just because your family may or may not have been involved doesn't mean you're guilty as well."

Amanda paused, thinking, then nodded. "At this point, I've got nothing to lose by digging my heels in, because I've got nowhere to go and no family except the memories I have of a handful of people I once knew." She looked into her nearly empty coffee cup. "Or thought I knew. I just feel like my back's against the wall, and it's time for me to really fight. If I'm going to build a life anywhere, then I need to start right now."

"No time like the present. And you'll want to eat that roll while it's still warm. They're best that way."

Amanda smiled and took a bite. Delicious, warm and buttery with loads of icing and cinnamon. Amazing!

Meg was obviously still thinking over their conversation. "If I were you I'd see what I could discover myself. Nobody has as much to lose as you do." Her eyes brightened and she clapped her hands together softly, obviously having hatched a brand new idea. "I think you need to talk to Mrs. Granger. She knows just about everything that's happened in this town for the last fifty years. Look, she may not know all the details, but I'd bet she'd point you in the right direction to find some answers."

"Who's Mrs. Granger?"

Meg chuckled a bit. "Think of her as kind of like Yoda, but with knowledge of the gossip on every single person in this town, probably. Picture the most ancient person you've ever met. She's so old she's got nothing to lose, and absolutely no filters on anything she says. She'll tell you anything she knows, whether you want to hear it or not, and she probably has some old photos of the Inn, from when it was in its heyday. She helps out the local historical society sometimes."

Amanda set down her plate, intrigued. "Do you think she'd mind if I visited so I could talk with her?"

Meg grinned. "She'd love it, but you don't need to visit her at home. I dropped her off at Petrie's general store this morning. Most days she spends her time on the bench by the woodstove, knitting and eavesdropping." Meg took another sip of coffee and then explained, "You'd be amazed at the stuff she hears in that place. Lots of people think because she's really old her hearing's bad or she's not very sharp, but they couldn't be more wrong. If they had any idea what she actually knew they'd never open their mouths around her again."

Amanda laughed and for the first time in hours she started to feel hopeful. Maybe it was the mocha or maybe it was the cinnamon roll, but she was pretty sure it was the feeling that someone was interested in her troubles enough to get her pointed in the right direction. Apparently, that direction was toward Mrs. Granger.

Meg got up and brushed the crumbs off her apron. "Let me wrap up a cinnamon roll for you to take to her. She normally just eats the bologna and pickle sandwiches that Brian makes for her at noon, but she loves the pastries I bake."

Amanda picked up her empty plate and cup, and brought them to the counter while Meg boxed up a huge roll.

"Just make sure she has her teeth in securely, okay?" Meg added, as she handed the box carefully across the display case. Amanda took it, with the feeling like it was meant to be an offering to some wise hermit.

"You know this much about everybody in this town, Meg?"

Her new friend shook her head, grinning. "Only when they're my grandmother."

Chapter 10

It was easy to find Mrs. Granger inside the general store, and Meg had been spot on when she described her as Yoda. She was a little cotton-haired lady of indeterminate age and shape, sitting on a padded wooden bench near an antique stove, her four-wheeled walker parked close by. Quietly knitting fingerless gloves by the light of the large window next to her, she was obviously eavesdropping on a lively conversation at the checkout register ten feet away.

"Mrs. Granger?" Amanda asked. She held the pink cinnamon roll box in her hands, waiting.

"Shhhhh! Just a minute..."

Amanda shifted foot to foot while the checker wrapped up her conversation with the chatty customer, and thanked her as she headed out the door.

With a satisfied sigh, the old lady settled back on the bench. "Now, what can I do for you, dear?"

Amanda held out the box. "Meg said I should come talk to you, and she sent over some pastries."

The toady little woman's eyes lit up, and she made excited "ooo" sounds as she grabbed the box.

"Have a seat!" She gestured vaguely at the wooden bench next to her as she pried open the lid and dug into the fat cinnamon roll.

"Sorry to shush you, but I was listening to Mary Anne Bates tell Myrna about her new Chrysler." Her voice dropped to a conspiratorial whisper. "You know, she's not a bad person, except she forgets to vote and she does grow the marijuana down in her chicken shed." Mrs. Granger pulled a huge piece of icing off the top of the roll and waved it at Amanda. "I don't like that. It's not healthy," she said, as she expertly crammed the chunk of frosting into her mouth.

After a couple minutes of enthusiastic chewing, she came up for air and smiled at Amanda. "You're the lady with the problem buried under her scarecrow, or rather, the problem that *was* buried under your scarecrow."

"You know about that?"

"Oh honey, I read the paper like a good taxpayer should. I'm figurin' you probably came to ask me about how Emmett wound up in your garden, six feet under."

"Um, it was more like three."

"Whatever."

Amanda shifted, uncomfortable. "Meg said you knew everything that had happened in this town for years, and I was hoping you had some ideas about who I should talk to."

Mrs. Granger kept her eyes on the next hunk of cinnamon roll, but she was obviously thinking. "You're wanting to know if your uncle killed Emmett, that's what you were hopin' to find out."

It was the truth but it still stung. "Mrs. Granger, do you know why my uncle and aunt left Ravenwood overnight? No one seems to know the details and after talking to the cops, it sounds like my family is the number one suspect."

The old lady's eyebrows went up. "I'm not surprised. Talk around town was that Emmett had a thing for your aunt, and he wasn't exactly the sorta guy who took rejection very well. He put his own sister in the hospital after smacking her around when she turned him down for a loan once, or so the story goes."

"Is there anyone one else who would've wanted him dead?"

Mrs. Granger snorted. "Who *wouldn't* want that boy dead? He'd had bad business dealings with all sorts of people and chased anything that wore a skirt. Do you know he once tried to run over Owen Winter's cat down by the oyster-processing plant? On purpose?" She waved her chunk of cinnamon roll for emphasis, heedless of the bits of frosting flying everywhere. "What sort of jackass tries to run over someone's poor cat?"

The old lady took a big bite, chewed a moment, then added, "No one in town liked him, and I'm on that list, too. Sounds like someone finally gave him a major attitude adjustment. Want some hot apple cider? Brian put a kettleful on the stove for me today."

Amanda shook her head and sighed, sensing defeat. "Do you know anyone else I should talk to about this, to try to clear my uncle's name?"

Mrs. Granger paused and cleared her throat, hesitating for a moment. "Maybe it wasn't your uncle. Maybe it was your aunt."

Amanda felt a flash of anger, but it was hard to be mad at the little old lady, especially when she might be right.

"Maybe." It was an admission, and it hurt. "The police haven't said what the cause of death is yet."

Mrs. Granger brushed crumbs off her velour tracksuit. "Well, we can be sure of one thing. No one with a head cold or appendicitis winds up down a three-foot deep hole by accident."

Amanda could feel the headache gathering between her eyes. "True. I talked to the detective on the case and he says I can't do any work on certain parts of the Inn until they complete their investigation, and I don't know what I'm going to do. I can't afford to just live in that place. I need it to be a business."

"Detective? Was it James Landon?" At Amanda's confirming nod, Mrs. Granger continued. "He was a wild one, that boy was. He's got three of the biggest, craziest brothers you'd ever meet and I guess he had to keep up with 'em. Got a sweet sister, though. You know James once got caught putting the principal's VW on top of the high school and just about didn't graduate? Would've been a shame. That boy read almost every book in the library." Her eyes sparkled a bit as she leaned over. "Not bad on the eyes either, doncha know."

Trying not to grin, Amanda didn't rise to the bait. "I didn't notice." What a liar she was.

Mrs. Granger scoffed. "Oh, I doubt that statement. I may be old, but I ain't dead, and I still notice."

Amanda decided to change the subject, even if it hurt to say the words.

"I met with Charles Timmins this morning and he seemed to imply that Emmett was having an affair, or wanted to have an affair, with my aunt."

"Hah! That boy wouldn't know crap from Crisco. You know he had to cheat at his classes just so he could pass law school?" She shook her finger at Amanda. "Used to date any girl who'd look at him, too, and take them up to his family's flour mill at nighttime and do God only knows what to them up there."

"Mrs. Granger, do you know if that's true?"

"And he leaves his dog's business in his neighbor's yard, when he should be using a baggie."

Amanda waited, and finally the old lady sighed, defeated. She closed the pink pastry box, carefully choosing her words.

"There were rumors, but truthfully I just don't know. I liked your Aunt Judy, and I never saw her do anything but work hard and keep her head down around here. She never spoke an ill word about anyone. She didn't let people know much about her personal life, and maybe she had reasons to not talk about it, but I just don't know."

Amanda thought back on her own past and her own private life. She could understand why her aunt may have wanted to keep things to herself, especially if she knew how quickly gossip could spread in a small town.

Mrs. Granger apparently disagreed. "I don't like secrets. Everybody has too many of them around here. People would be much happier if they could just live their lives honestly, out in the open."

Her gaze was unwavering when she leaned over again and told Amanda seriously, "Secrets kill people."

Chapter 11

Amanda hadn't expected visitors before breakfast. She certainly didn't expect a gift of a dead mouse, square on her welcome mat, and the first thing she saw when she stepped outside in the morning. She gave a little yelp of surprise as she sidestepped the rodent, and then she heard a soft meow. The same striped orange cat she'd seen before, huge and too thin, was sitting on one of the top railings of the covered porch, watching her carefully and not moving.

Amanda looked at the dead offering by her feet and sighed. "Is this a gift from you?" The cat blinked and didn't answer. "Look, kitty, you can have all the tuna you want, but just don't leave me any more little presents first thing in the morning, okay?"

Pretending that the mousey wasn't there, she settled into a cane chair she'd put on the broad porch. It had become her favorite place to eat breakfast, watching the quiet country road out front of the Inn, and out of the weather. Today looked to be fair and bright, and she wouldn't need her umbrella. She was starting to get used to the vagaries of the Oregon coast weather, where a bright spot of sunshine could be followed by a downpour five minutes later. Sunshine was always welcomed as an unexpected blessing.

Maybe the nice weather's a good omen, she thought, and took a sip of her coffee. The big cat settled into a sphinx-like position on the railing, pretending to be asleep but periodically peeking at her through half-closed eyes. "I see you," Amanda informed him, to which her visitor only yawned widely. "It looks like you could do with a better diet than mice." The cat's green eyes opened, as if it understood exactly what she'd said. "You wait right there and I'll see if I can find you something to eat in the kitchen."

***

After she'd fed the cat and her new furry guest had used his rough tongue to scrape every last bit of tuna from the plate, Amanda spent a few hours cleaning up after the police and their thorough search of the Inn. Straightening furniture and drawers, she tucked away paperwork and rearranged anything that she knew had been moved. It was a productive and satisfying task, but really she was just killing time before the big event of the day.

Finally, she couldn't wait any longer, so she dug through her luggage for her best business clothes and spent some extra time on her makeup and hair. A quick search of the laundry room turned up an electric iron and a cloth-covered board, so she got to work making sure her clothes were in perfect shape. If she was going to dig in her heels in this town, she might as well look her best.

She'd done a lot of thinking about how to deal with the mayor's reaction to her opening the Inn, and slowly realized that there had been things done in secret. Maybe what was needed was some out-in-the-open public conversation. Today was the biweekly city council meeting and she had decided to attend, whether they wanted her there or not. It definitely wasn't in her comfort zone, but the town and the Inn had both grown on her, even if they hadn't been exactly easy and friendly at first. This was her home, and she was going to fight for it.

Trying to control her jitters, she tucked her notepad and a new pen into her purse so she'd be able to organize her thoughts a bit better. In her last job she'd given more than her share of presentations to the management so she was used to building a case to persuade others. Over and over she had to show the executives just how effective her little team of fraud detectives was against the people who wanted to file fake claims just to get insurance payouts. Hopefully, that experience would help her present a clear reason for reopening the Ravenwood Inn.

You think I'd be calm about this, she thought but she knew this time was different. This was for something much bigger than a bit of pride or to show off a team. This town council meeting could make or break her new business, and could change the way her whole life would go.

The old wooden Grange hall was open, the front door propped in place with a wedge doorstop, and a few people filtering in under the big barn lights. The large room was full of folding metal chairs, most of them empty with just a handful of townspeople finding a place to sit and chatting together in little groups.

Amanda spotted several people she knew, including the reporter Lisa Wilkins, who was talking to her barista friend, Meg. Amanda threaded her way through the rows of chairs to the front of the room to take a seat by her.

"I really enjoyed meeting your grandmother, Meg. She's a kick!"

Meg laughed in agreement. "Yeah, she's something alright. She said she liked you, too. Said you had gumption, whatever that means."

"I'm kind of scared to ask what it means."

"Don't be. She's as good a judge of character as anyone you'll ever meet. If she said something like that about you, it only means you're a good person who interests her. That's all."

Amanda looked around the room, at the scrubbed wooden walls with photos of long-dead townspeople, and at the simply-dressed crowd slowly filing in. She felt about a million miles away from her former life in LA, where she hardly ever talked to people who weren't in her age group or her circle of friends and coworkers. Back there, the whole tone of her day could be set by whether she got her favorite coffee specialty drink before she dragged herself into work.

They waited quietly until the three council members, including Mayor Sandford, solemnly filed in from a side door and sat behind the long table on the stage. As soon as they'd been seated, the crowd became absolutely silent, as if the presence of the officials alone had somehow snuffed the joy out of the room.

Watching the small council conduct business, it became instantly apparent that they weren't impressed with the proposals before them, and that every request was quickly voted down. A proposal for a new greenhouse to be built at the side of Petrie's hardware store was immediately quashed, with the admonition that Petrie's was a historic building that shouldn't have any changes made to it. The middle-school principal stood up to present her case for the purchase of a newer bus to collect children from the nearby town of Likely, and the vote was once again a unanimous no, citing lack of funding. There was a bit of grumbling from the townspeople as they shifted uncomfortably in their seats, but no one offered any objections.

"The man on the council is actually a renter of Mrs. Sandford's, and he's deathly afraid of her," Meg whispered to Amanda. "In all the time he's been on the council, I've never seen him vote differently than Mrs. Sandford on *anything*."

"What about the lady?" Amanda asked, pointing toward the plump matron dressed in gray, who was carefully studying her nails.

"Betty Monroe. Some sort of cousin of Mrs. Sandford's dead husband. Rumor has it that she's been borrowing money from Sandford for years. God only knows how much she actually owes her."

So much for an impartial hearing.

Amanda leaned over and whispered, "I've never heard of a town named Likely. Is it close to Ravenwood Cove?"

Meg scoffed. "It's about seven miles east of here, up in the hills with only one main road in and out. You definitely don't want to go visit. Lots of trailer homes with tarps over the roofs, and the cops know just about every family there by name. It can be kinda rough sometimes."

Lisa added, "We always said that if something bad was going to happen, it was likely going to happen at Likely."

After working through their agenda, Mrs. Sandford set her black purse on the table, pulled on her gloves and asked if anyone had new business to discuss. *Can't wait to get out of here,* Amanda thought, and raised her hand.

"Yes, actually, I do," she said, and saw a flash of disappointment flicker across the Mayor's face. Mrs. Sandford sighed and sat down, her gloves still in place, as she gestured for the younger woman to speak.

Amanda had been practicing the words in her head all morning, and they still came out in a tumble. She laid out who she was, how she'd inherited the Inn, and the steps she was taking to bring it back to its former glory. She told them her plans and how she was willing to go through the proper steps to be sure that the building would be an asset to the town and the neighborhood, all while preserving its history and character. Her last statement was an impassioned plea for the city council to change the zoning back to its original designation so she could open for business and accept guests again.

By the time she came up for breath, she could hear murmurs of agreement from the townspeople, and see the look of open disapproval on the mayor's face.

"I think we've certainly heard enough about the Inn lately, Miss Graham." She drew Amanda's name out with the same tone that she would've used on a disruptive child. "One only has to read the papers to see what is truly happening at the Inn. With such sordid goings-on, I am certain the town doesn't need the type of excitement that your business would entail."

Amanda was trying to keep her temper, but Meg could definitely tell it was a struggle and she put a gentle hand on her friend's arm as the mayor kept speaking.

"With the nature of the town becoming more mature and peaceful, it is the council's decision that reopening the Ravenwood Inn to anyone who wants to visit would not fit with the local climate of tranquility. It also does not adhere to the current regulations regarding short-term rentals. Thus, your proposal to reopen and rezone is vetoed."

"Don't you even want to pretend that the other council members have a say?" someone asked. The mayor quickly conferred with the other people at her table, and they both popped their hands up in support of the mayor's position.

Amanda could feel her future slipping away. "Look, I'm not asking for special treatment. I'm not here to upset the town or do anything that hasn't already been done before. The Ravenwood Inn has decades of elegant and honorable history in this town, and has been a haven for visitors and travelers. I'm not trying to make it into a Motel 6. I want it to be what it was before, elegant and beautiful." Her voice was almost wistful.

"I'm sorry, but that simply won't be possible." The mayor's voice was calm, and if Amanda hadn't known better she'd almost say it was soothing.

That was it. The gloves came off.

"Mayor Sandford, can you tell me why *you* were the one to request that the Ravenwood Inn be made into a residence?"

The mayor had the grace to look confused. "I'm sure I don't know what you mean, Miss Graham."

Amanda did her best to keep her voice calm and strong. "I saw the assessor's records, Mayor. They show that the Inn has been rezoned for residential use only. It also shows that you were the one to request the change, the very day we first met."

Mrs. Sandford's eyebrows shot up in surprise. "Well, I'm sure I don't know what you're babbling about, Miss Graham, but it sounds like the assessor has seen the wisdom of having consistent zoning for that area, which is individual houses. I applaud his decision."

Amanda pulled herself to her feet, ignoring Meg's softly hissed warning to keep calm. "Well, if I can't open to guests, how about I just host murder-mystery nights?" Her voice was raising and getting louder and she didn't care at all. "I could do those wine-tasting parties where people can follow clues and try to figure whodunit and why. Maybe give them tours of my garden and the six-foot long hole in it and sell postcards of my scarecrow. How about *them* apples?"

There was no mistaking the look of rage on the mayor's face, or the wide open mouths of the other two council members. "This meeting is adjourned!" Mrs. Sanford spat out as she banged her gavel loudly on the table and stalked quickly from the room.

It was hard not to cry, either from frustration or disappointment, and Amanda knew she'd also ruined any chance she'd have for future relations with the council by goading them with the idea of holding murder mystery parties at the Inn. Truthfully, she'd only said it in anger, but the horrified looks on their faces almost made her want to do it to spite them.

Meg kept her voice low. "Well, I think that's the sort of thing my Gramma meant when she mentioned you had gumption."

Meg and Lisa didn't say much else as they patted Amanda on the back and picked up their jackets to walk out with her. Head down, Amanda barely caught a glimpse of a familiar dark jacket out of the corner of her eye, moving to intersect them.

"Detective Landon. You always show up at city council meetings?"

His grin was broad and infectious. "Only if there promises to be fireworks. Did you come here just to make Mayor Sandford clutch her double strand of pearls in horror? If so, you did a good job of it."

Meg tried not to laugh as Amanda rolled her eyes. "Sometimes things just come out, okay? She made me mad and now she's going to make me bankrupt. She deserved any pearl clutching she got."

The tall detective leaned a bit closer, his eyes locked with hers. "Remind me to stay on your good side, lady."

Amanda caught a faint whiff of something masculine and clean, like good leather or fresh pine. Aftershave. Or maybe it was just the testosterone.

Whatever it was, it was definitely affecting her concentration level.

Amanda missed the silent message Lisa and Meg were telegraphing to each other behind her, but Meg understood it perfectly. "Well, Lisa and I have got to be going. We'll catch up to you later. Bye!" and before Amanda could protest, her two friends were scuttling out the side door. Standing alone with the detective in the hall, she watched the last stragglers filing out of the room.

"I may have some information that could help. How about a cup of coffee?" His face was serious, but his eyes were sparkling with mischief, as if he was keeping fun secrets.

"Actually, I really need food." Amanda could tell the adrenaline from her confrontation was beginning to fade, and her knees felt a bit shaky. "Know a good place to get a sandwich?"

Chapter 12

It was less than a five-minute walk to Ivy's Café, a cheerful little restaurant tucked onto Main Street behind a dark green awning, kitty-corner from Petrie's Hardware and directly across from Kazoodles toy store. James smiled and nodded at several customers as they walked in, obviously in his element. The sign said "Seat Yourself", so Amanda settled into a booth by the windows gratefully and looked over the menu the smiling waitress handed her.

"You don't need that."

She pulled her menu down a bit, and saw James' serious expression. She'd almost believe it, except that his short-cropped dark hair was sticking up in all directions and it gave him the appearance of a puckish boy. It was both careless and masculine, but it still made her suppress a chuckle.

"They make the best bacon cheeseburgers in the *world*, and the most amazing clam chowder you'll ever eat. Ivy's is known all over for those two things. Trust me, they're fantastic."

"What if I'm a vegan?"

He snorted in disgust. "Then you're gonna starve in this town, lady."

Amanda couldn't help but laugh. "A bacon cheeseburger sounds great."

Two orders for cheeseburgers, and the waitress hurried away, humming happily. Amanda looked out the window at the little shops and people walking by on the wide sidewalks. If she didn't know better, it looked deceptively calm and old-fashioned. Too bad she'd seen such a bad side of Ravenwood Cove since she'd arrived because, truthfully, she'd rather have never known that such a side existed.

"Sounds like you know a lot about the people in this town, Detective. Come here often?"

He chuckled; a deep, rich sound. "It hasn't changed much since I was a boy. The people who live here have stayed because they like that continuity." He followed her gaze across the street. "I can remember taking every dime of my allowance down to Kazoodles on Saturday morning, just to see what I could get." He took a sip of his coffee. "Still get toys and gifts for my nieces there."

Amanda looked out the window and sighed. "Looks like a normal little town, doesn't it? Too bad a crazy lady runs it."

"She's not crazy, but she does have her way of thinking about things, and I think people just got tired of fighting her. She can be an immovable object sometimes. "

"Well, maybe that means I have to be the irresistible force, I guess."

He grinned. "No comment, but you're definitely kinda stubborn."

"You said you had some information for me?" Amanda studiously ignored his jab.

They paused and leaned back while the waitress slid two huge platters of food in front of them, smiling warmly at the detective while she pulled a ketchup bottle out of her apron pocket and plunked it onto the table.

"Will there be anything else?"

"No, thanks, Ruby."

Amanda watched the trim waitress walk away, and couldn't help but ask.

"Um, friend of yours?"

James took an enormous bite of his burger and nodded.

"Thought so," Amanda said, and tried the burger, too. It *was* amazing.

"I've known her family for years, and we went to high school together. When you grow up in a small town you get to know just about everybody."

Amanda had a brief mental flash of what her companion must've looked like in high school, but suppressed it. Football player? Prom king? She could certainly picture him with cheerleaders hanging off his muscular arm.

"What did you want to talk about?"

His face was deadly serious as he leaned forward.

"Look, what we talk about here today needs to stay here, okay? This info doesn't get talked around town or show up in the paper or get discussed with girlfriends."

Amanda bristled. "I'd never do that."

"Pinky swear?"

She laughed and took the proffered pinky, linking it with hers, making a pact with him. "Pinky swear. I'll be good."

"Just a couple things you should know. First, it was definitely Emmett Johnson buried in your garden. Dental records confirm it, so at least that gives us something to go on."

Amanda's breath caught in her throat. Her mystery now had a real name, and a real face. "How did he die?"

James paused and set down his burger. "I hate to admit it, but we're really not sure. There was no sign of trauma to the body or bullets, and no bones that looked like they'd been broken before death. We'll keep working on finding an answer to that, but right now we got nothin'."

She shivered, her thoughts instantly going to her uncle and the argument he'd had with Emmett.

"Anything else?"

James nodded. "Forensics found a folded piece of paper in his wallet, but it was unreadable. They also found a chalky substance all over the remains and inside the lungs, but it hasn't been identified yet. Oh, and the tape used to tape the plastic shut is the packing tape that Petrie's hardware has custom-made, with their logo on it. They use it to help wrap bulky purchases or seal mail order boxes."

"Petrie's?" She thought of Brian, the helpful man who'd kept his store open late just to be sure she'd had lanterns and bug spray. He seemed so nice. "Does that make the owner a suspect?"

"Until we narrow it down I can't officially say, but I can tell you that Emmett probably had lots of people who wanted to kill him. He wasn't exactly an upstanding sort of guy."

"Will your investigation results be in the paper?"

James shook his head, swallowing a bite of his lunch. "Not usually. Well, maybe some of them. A lot of times we don't release all our info to the press because it could tip our hand, or because the details are too gruesome to print for the public."

She shuddered. Too gruesome. Maybe sometimes it was better not to know the details of murders and mayhem.

Amanda's mind whirled with the possibilities and the clues. It was almost too much to take, so she switched to a safer subject.

"You wanted to talk about the mayor?"

"Not necessarily the mayor, but what the plans are for the town. Did you know that the Crescent Crown Company is looking at buying the forested acreage about a half block north of you? The one on the bluff with the panoramic view of the cove?"

She knew that land; a huge crescent of bluff with patches of tall trees. "Yes, I think I know it."

The detective continued. "Well, you're sure not going to like this. Guess who owns that particular piece of gorgeous and valuable real estate."

Amanda could feel her stomach twist with sudden dread. "You mean the mayor?"

He nodded. "It's been in her family for generations, and now she's the legal owner."

"What's the Crescent Crown Company?"

He hesitated, almost sorry to put the pieces of the puzzle together for her. "It's one of the biggest retirement resort companies in the country. They go around buying up very expensive and desirable chunks of land so they can build super-luxurious resorts on them, catering only to wealthy retirees."

Amanda gulped, her mind racing. "You mean the mayor…"

He nodded, seeing she was on the right track. "She stands to make millions if that deal goes through. They want her land."

"What about the Inn?"

"Your property is right next to hers. If the resort company decided to expand, your land would be worth a fortune. They have a history of buying up surrounding properties and putting in more condos."

"But only if the town…"

"Stays off the beaten path. That means exclusive, private, no tourists, no weekend rentals, no new roads or businesses coming in that won't directly benefit the retirement community. Crescent Crown is famous for its requirements of the surrounding areas, as their members want only the best. I wouldn't be surprised if they would want to update the local shops with something bigger and more modern."

"Like what?"

"Let's just say they're known for pushing the local people to allow in huge companies that have contracts exclusively with them, and ones that will give the resort residents steep discounts."

Amanda's mouth dropped open, thinking of Cuppa and Kazoodles and Petrie's Hardware and all the small businesses in town.

"James, I've heard about companies that do that kind of thing. That will wipe out almost every shop owner in town. Does anyone else know about this yet?"

"Not yet. I don't have any solid data to give you right now, but I'll see what I can pull together. You understand that as an officer of the law I can't officially take sides on this."

Amanda's face registered surprise. "You can't take sides but you're telling me all this?"

James tried to look innocent and failed entirely. "I've lived here my whole life and I'm not willing to let Ravenwood just die due to corporate greed. Let's just say that I think you may be a person who'd have an interest in doing something about Crescent Crown. I think that if you got a chance you might figure out that this little town is exactly the sort of place you need,

Miss Graham, and that there are people here who you could actually get to know a bit."

"It has been nice making friends here," Amanda admitted. "There didn't seem to be many people I could talk to in LA."

The handsome detective leaned over and put his broad, warm hand over hers. "You can always talk to me."

Too much. It was too much to expect her to get involved with someone just because he was giving her the info she needed to try to change her circumstances. She'd always prided herself on being able to stand on her own two feet, on being able to walk away when things got too complex or ugly, and she'd certainly seen ugly up close and personal with the last man in her life.

She reluctantly pulled her hand away and picked up her burger, trying to control her breathing so he wouldn't know that her heart was racing.

"Thank you, Detective. If I have anything to report, I'll be sure to contact you."

Best to keep things impersonal, she thought, even though she read the disappointment in his grey-green eyes.

"I'd appreciate that, Miss Graham." His voice was cool, efficient. "Any assistance you can provide to the authorities would be helpful."

They ate in silence, all the while wondering what the other was thinking, and trying not to dribble ketchup on their chins.

Chapter 13

Even if her time at Ivy's with James hadn't been very comfortable, the information he had given her was a goldmine, and certainly got her motivated.

The news about the mayor and the retirement community had really ticked her off. There'd been a murder in town, and all she's interested in is her own profit and turning this place into some sort of retirement haven? Whether she was in it for her own profit or some other reasons really didn't matter. The bottom line was her selfishness was hurting everyone, including the owner of the Ravenwood Inn.

Was the mayor trying to devalue the Inn enough to buy it from Amanda, or did she have some other plan in mind? Either way, the thought of giving up the Inn after so much work and intrigue made Amanda's stomach hurt. Sure, at first the thought of just fixing it up to sell it may have been at the back of her mind, but with each day that she'd been working on it, she'd been able to see the potential beauty in the old building, and in Ravenwood Cove itself. Yes, it wasn't LA, but she was starting to see a glimmer of what her future could be in a small town where everyone knew everyone, and she was beginning to like that image.

The question was, what did she do now? She puzzled over this as she drove slowly back to the Inn, thinking back on James' words and trying to figure out what to do about it.

How can she prove the link to the mayor? Would it hurt the town if she told them about the upcoming real estate deal, or would it benefit the merchants to know about what was being plotted against them? Amanda wasn't sure. If she told the secret that she knew, maybe to Lisa at the newspaper, she might be doing more harm than good. Telling the merchants about the Crescent Crown Company might panic them into selling, and that was the last thing she wanted for this little town.

Either she was going to have to find a way to change the mayor's mind, and she didn't think she could do that, or she was going to have to think outside the box and come up with a different plan. A plan to help the merchants, attract tourists so the resort company didn't want to build in this town, and hopefully save the Ravenwood Inn. She was in too deep to back down now.

By the time she'd parked in the circular driveway, a plan was beginning to form. The moment she was back inside the Inn, Amanda opened her laptop on the kitchen island and got to work.

The new cat had definitely made himself at home, seemingly thrilled to have his own food bowl and a human servant who would fill it on command. He rubbed against Amanda's ankles and when that didn't get him the attention he wanted, he hopped onto the counter, content to just sit and purr as Amanda typed like crazy.

She'd been used to putting together websites for past projects so she knew a bit about software and design, and by the end of the day she had two very professional-looking websites up on the internet.

The first one she created was for the Ravenwood Inn, and included historic photos of it in its heyday, as well as a blog detailing the restoration efforts she was attempting. She made sure to include a glowing review of Roy Greeley's construction company, and put in the recent article the newspaper had done about the remodel. At first she was tempted to include information about the discovery of Emmett Johnson under her scarecrow but she finally decided not to. Even if he was universally disliked, she wasn't the sort to profit off of someone else's death, and she certainly didn't want any more questions or pointing fingers about her uncle's possible involvement. She wanted good publicity, not notoriety.

The second website took her more time and thought, because it was for her new hometown, Ravenwood Cove. She was lucky to be able to snap up the domain because it looked like no one else had ever thought of starting a website to feature the local business and the charm of the beach town. Using the best photos she could find, both new and historic, she included links to any merchant websites she could find. Many of the local shops didn't have their own sites on the internet, so she put together simple descriptions for them, making a note to talk to the owners for more info later. She wanted to be sure they were happy with their new web presence and with what she was doing. As she typed and made to do lists and uploaded everything, her mind was working through possibilities of how to help the town, and ways to get her beautiful Inn open again.

And that's how she thought of her place. Beautiful. The quiet building, steeped in years of dignity and the laughter and comfort of guests, had really grown on her as she had peeled off the layers of neglect and disuse. She genuinely loved the curve of the main staircase, the broad rooms with their comfortable and carved furniture, and the view of colorful sunsets from her balconies. Yes, maybe she did have a crazy rooster that woke her up every morning at dawn by crowing his head off somewhere down her little street, and maybe her neighbors were flat-out weird, but the quirkiness of this place was starting to almost seem normal.

If there were any ghosts here, they seemed to be just ghosts of happy memories. As long as she didn't think too much about the hole in the garden, Amanda was able to almost see the loving couples waltzing around the parlor on a long ago summer's night. The more she worked on the websites, the more those hopeful thoughts coalesced in her mind. This was a life worth fighting for. It was hers, and she was going to do what she had to in order to keep it.

So the townspeople were interested in her and what was going on with the Inn?

FINE. If they were interested in her she was going to make sure they knew she was interested in them. The websites might help a bit, but she knew that a couple small sites would be nearly impossible to find among so many websites about the Oregon coast. Why would someone be interested in Ravenwood Cove in the first place?

She needed something else. She needed to find out what people were thinking about the current city council and what was going on.

***

The next morning she packed her purse with a pad of paper and extra pens, and headed to Main Street. Amanda parked and looked down the sidewalk, seeing the tiny little shops, some with apartments on the second story for the owners, stretching out toward the town square with its tall flagpole. The chill of the morning fog clung to her as she stepped out of her car and scanned the quiet street. Under cheerful storefronts and awnings, shop owners were just starting to turn over OPEN signs, water the big hanging pots of late season flowers hanging from the antique streetlamps, and sweep stray leaves from their doorsteps. A couple of merchants set out bowls of fresh water for any dogs that strolled by.

The marquee on the theater boasted that it was running a classic movie, Lawrence of Arabia, for just three dollars. She could hear the jingle of the bell over the door in Petrie's when Brian stepped outside, broom in hand. He spotted her and gave her a broad wave.

Packing tape, she thought. *How did his packing tape get wrapped around a corpse in my garden?*

She waved back, trying to give her best smile and turned toward Cuppa. If she was going to talk with Mr. Petrie, it would have to be after she'd had a lot of coffee and a bit more courage.

Amanda spent her morning walking from shop to shop, waiting her turn while the friendly owners helped other customers and then chatting with them. They seemed moderately happy but almost skeptical when she told them about the new website she'd built for the town, and when Amanda started asking questions, it didn't take long for a common theme to emerge. Grace TwoHorses at Kazoodles said the same exact sort of thing that Tory Sherwood, the owner of Cuppa, expressed. They loved their little town, they wanted to stay and keep their business there, but times were tough and there just weren't enough customers to keep them open forever.

"It's like the town is drying up," Grace said as she arranged the front window display, full of elaborate Lego dioramas that the local kids had created.

"Have you ever met up with the other business owners and talked about this?" Amanda asked. "Maybe there's something you could do if you band together."

"Why bother? It's not like we're going to get more people into town to buy stuff anyway."

Amanda thought about that, watching while Grace stepped back to view the elaborate display, a look of satisfaction on her face.

"What if we could get more people to come to town?"

Grace scoffed, not unkindly, as she walked back toward the counter. "Yeah, good luck with that," she said. "See how many customers we have?" She gestured to the empty store. "It'd have to be something pretty drastic to get more people in here. I do my best but no matter how many sales I run or how great that front window looks, if people aren't visiting town there's no one to buy anything." She plopped down on the wooden stool behind the cash register. "I can't make a living selling just to the locals. At this rate, I'll have to close up shop before Christmas."

From the butcher, Jeff Prudhoe to the baker, Mrs. Mason, the response was pretty much the same. She listened carefully to everyone's frustrations and concerns, nodding her head and sympathizing, and being sure to buy something at every store. Maybe it was just a small, silly gesture but she wanted to help, and she wanted them to know she appreciated what they were going through.

Madeline Wu, the owner of the local fish store, wrapped up two pounds of her best salmon and refused to take payment for it when Amanda tried to hand her a twenty. "On the house. Welcome to Ravenwood Cove!" Madeline said, smiling warmly and passing over the fish, now wrapped with an ice pack in white butcher paper. Amanda almost felt guilty taking it but after a bit of protesting, she thanked Madeline and asked for ideas on how to cook it. By the time she walked out she had a great new recipe for a blackberry glaze for the fish, and had seen at least a dozen photos of Madeline's grandchildren, all proudly displayed in a little album she kept under the front counter.

It was about noontime and Amanda's tummy was rumbling for lunch. She tucked the fish and ice into her car, glad that she'd parked in the shade of one of the huge maples growing by the wide sidewalk, and headed to Ivy's café. She'd already begun to hatch a plan and as soon as she settled into a back booth at Ivy's she pulled out her notebook. After ordering a big bowl of clam chowder she began frantically jotting down ideas and details. It was going to be a challenge to try to come up with something that would help people and still wouldn't disclose the possible land sale to the retirement community developer. If she had to, she would do that as a last resort, but she was hoping to avoid the certain uproar and panic that would bring.

One thing was for sure; working on ideas to help the town's shopkeepers was helping her forget about her own troubles a bit. She couldn't change the fact that her family was under suspicion for murder, or that her own business was sinking like a rock, or that her bank account was rapidly drying up. At least she had a roof over her head, and some new friends, and a chance to help someone else.

So my own life is going straight into the dumpster, she thought, tasting the soup. *Maybe I've been thinking too much about myself.* She couldn't remember the last time she'd really gone out on a limb to help someone who wasn't close friends or family.

James was right. The chowder was amazing. He lingered in her thoughts as she ate, and she wondered what he was doing about the investigation into Emmett's murder. She wasn't used to trusting other people, but she knew in this case she'd have to.

I'll touch base with him later, she thought, with a pang of regret. *I've got other things to do.*

Chapter 14

It was worth getting up so early. Anger definitely felt better than despair, and Amanda gripped her backpack and shovel tightly as she locked up her car in the empty parking lot.

She didn't mind the dampness of the fog or the soft darkness of the pre-dawn morning. Once she'd walked through the whip-like seagrass toward the ocean, the empty beach stretched on either side of her for miles. A constant wind nearly muffled the sound of the rolling surf, white with constantly-moving foam, crashing against the shore in timeless rhythm. She pulled out her spade and got to work, a few seagulls hovering nearly motionless overhead in case she'd brought food. Setting her mouth in a grim line of determination, Amanda thought about her plan and how it might play out.

Starting to dig, she focused on the tiny holes and bubbles in the sand, and the reflection of gray sky and green water. Simple and beautiful, and here since ages before people ever walked this beach.

She'd already been working for about fifteen minutes and made several holes when she heard the crunching sound of footsteps on the sand and the scent of a familiar aftershave let her know she wasn't alone. The seagulls winged off without any sense of panic, in search of quieter hunting grounds.

"What do you think you're doing?" Detective Landon sounded more curious than accusatory.

She kept digging, her spade making deep cuts as she shoveled the sand out of the hole.

"I'm planting."

She heard his snort of dismissal. "Planting in the sand?"

"Well, for some odd reason I don't feel like planting stuff in my garden anymore."

He ignored her pathetic joke, peeking over her shoulder as she turned her body away from him a bit. Finishing her hole while he watched in silence, she leaned over to pull something out of the nearby backpack.

It was a seashell, huge and beautifully intricate, and definitely not from any sort of shellfish that had ever lived near Oregon. It had obviously come from some exotic tropical beach somewhere. James caught a glimpse of more shells in the bag.

Amanda smiled with satisfaction as she carefully placed the shell, as big as her hand, in the sandy hole, and used the spade to fill it in.

"They're from my aunt's collection," she finally explained as she picked up her pack and moved about ten feet away, starting a new hole as he followed. "She loved to travel and bring seashells home as souvenirs and I found boxes and boxes of them in the Inn. I'm just putting them back where they belong. I think she'd approve."

He watched her, still confused. "If I'm right, the shells you have in that bag were probably collected from beaches all over the world. Why are you putting them here?"

"I'm recycling."

"Um, technically, you're littering."

She looked up, her face showing her annoyance. "I am not. I'm just putting natural things back in a natural place."

She pulled a small glass fishing float out her pack and dropped it in the new hole. "See? That float probably came from around here. People find Japanese glass floats on the beach all the time."

James waited, knowing there had to be some sort of reasonable explanation why she was out in the pre-dawn chill, planting seashells and blue glass balls.

"Besides, what kid wouldn't want to find something like that when they start digging for a sandcastle?"

Her voice sounded deceptively Innocent, but the tone confirmed that she was definitely up to something. He mulled it over, trying to put the pieces together. It took him a full minute to start figuring out what his devious, clever, pain-in-the-backside friend was up to.

"You're doing this to get more kids to the beach, aren't you? Somehow you've got a plan to stick it to Mrs. Sandford and her goal to have this be a quiet retirement community." His mind was racing, trying to figure out her scheme. "What is it, Amanda? What have you got up your sleeve?"

She ignored him, carefully tamping down the sand on top of the newly-buried treasure, and smoothing the surface before she moved a few yards away and started a new hole. He followed her, still working on the question of what she was doing. It finally completely clicked into place, and his mouth dropped open for a moment before he blurted out his conclusion.

"You know that if a kid finds something like that, the word will get out eventually when more kids find big shells and stuff here. Maybe that means publicity for Ravenwood. That means more families will want to come stay and visit." He looked at her, wanting confirmation that he was on the right track.

"I don't know what you're talking about." She tried to sound innocent and completely failed. The sand crunched around her shovel as she continued to dig, and tossed in a white shell that looked like an angel wing.

His eyebrow arched over one eye as he leaned close to her face, and she darted her eyes away to avoid his gaze.

"Uh huh. *Right.* You've cooked up some scheme to get the word out, haven't you, Amanda?"

She kicked the last of the damp sand in the hole and straightened up, still clutching her shovel.

"Maybe. What if I did, Detective?" She looked him in the eye, defiant. "What if I'm tired of people telling me no all the time and telling me what to do and treating me like dirt? What if I think that I'd rather do something like this instead of..?"

"Instead of planting someone from the city council in your garden?"

She patted the loose sand at the top of the hole. "I'd never do that."

A deep sigh and then she gave a reluctant laugh. "Well, maybe the thought had crossed my mind," she finally admitted.

"So, this is your way to protest?"

She straightened up, wisps of her hair moving around her face in the morning wind. "You got a better idea, Detective? This town is dying, and my future is dying with it. If we're going to keep Ravenwood going we're going to have to fight back, and I certainly can't afford some court battle that would bankrupt me. I'd probably lose anyway because what the mayor's doing isn't against the law, technically. Tell me, is that justice?"

James thought about it, hearing the near-desperation in her voice. The idea of justice was one of the reasons he'd become a police officer in the first place, hoping to make a difference after he'd seen too many wrongs go unstopped and unpunished.

Amanda watched his face carefully. Finally, she pulled a huge conch shell out of the backpack and held it out to him, waiting. The shell was beautiful, coiled with white and gold, and with a soft blush of smooth Caribbean pink at the opening. It was nearly as big as her head.

"You wanna help?"

"You trying to get me kicked off the force?"

"Just trying to do the right thing, Detective. What about you?"

He hesitated for a moment, sighed deeply, and grabbed the conch. "Okay, lady, I'm in. Just don't go spreading this around town, okay?"

Amanda giggled gleefully and gave him a quick sideways hug. "It's our secret. I knew you'd help, though! Now get digging. We don't want to be out in daylight doing this."

"Yes, ma'am." His hug was warm and solid, and she tried to keep her grin hidden as they worked their way down the beach, digging hole after hole after hole.

Chapter 15

Within forty-eight hours the local paper was running a fat front page headline of RAVENWOOD COVE TREASURE HUNT, reporting on the new phenomenon of children digging in the sand and finding huge, exotic shells from around the globe. The reporter had interviewed six different kids who had been happy to pose for a photo and tell the story of how they'd discovered their treasure while building a sand castle or digging a hole. In the next edition of the paper, the Cuppa coffeehouse was offering a free chocolate chip cookie to any child that brought in their discovery, as well as promising to post their picture on the wall and to give their parents a complimentary book of coupons for discounts and freebies from most of the merchants in town.

By the next day the Oregonian newspaper, based in Portland, had picked up the story as a human interest feature and had sent a reporter down to get photos of the fun discoveries people were finding in Ravenwood Cove. The reporter interviewed the barista at Cuppa, and was there just in time to take photos of a bubbly seven-year-old with pigtails who had discovered a huge African cowrie while digging a sand fort. The photo of the cute grade-schooler, excitedly grinning a gap-toothed smile and holding up her free cookie and gorgeous seashell, was featured on the front of the Sunday travel section, along with several paragraphs of praise for the town's unspoiled beauty, historic architecture, and local crafts.

That night the websites for Ravenwood Cove and the Inn started getting email, with people asking questions about activities for families and places to stay. As much as it hurt to be sitting in her beautiful Inn and telling people that the nearest lodging was a small hotel seven miles down the road, Amanda did just that. She made sure to be welcoming and polite, telling the people about the great shops and the beautiful and uncrowded beach. She also asked if they'd like to be added to her newsletter, so they'd be the first to know when the Ravenwood Inn was open for guests.

The next morning, Mrs. Sandford had stomped down to the newspaper office and handed in a typed press release about a lice outbreak at the local school, and the proposed expansion of the sewage plant in the next town, Likely. Lisa hesitantly took the piece of paper the mayor thrust in front of her, scanning it quickly.

"Run it. I wanted it printed *today*."

The mayor spun on her heel and left without saying another word.

Lisa's reporter instincts were tingling as she read the paper, and the more she read, the more she understood that the mayor was doing her best to discourage people wanting to visit Ravenwood Cove. The information was mostly true, but the statements definitely made things sound much worse than they actually were. With each sentence, her anger rose. She remembered every bit of info that the mayor had told the newspaper to run or tried to suppress, and the constant battles Mr. Fields, the previous editor, had had with the fierce lady.

She didn't like it. In fact, she'd had just about enough of the mayor making decisions about the town and its people and economy that suited her own interests, without checking with the residents to see what *they* wanted. She'd watched her parents struggle to make a profit with the small charter fishing business they owned in Ravenwood, and lately every effort to expand or advertise had been thwarted by Mrs. Sandford.

Lisa thought of all the other shop owners she knew in town. She thought of their families and the kids she'd gone to school with, and the ones who had gone through rough times, trying to keep their business afloat. Something inside her snapped. It was time to take some action.

She flipped open her laptop and got to work. The editorial poured out of her, and by the time she got to the words 'dictatorial' and 'imperious' she was grinning and feeling like a rogue pirate. She'd never gone this far out on a limb, but was ready for whatever fallout would happen, and it felt damn good to take a stand.

Freedom of the press, she thought smugly, and started putting together the articles to highlight her blasting editorial. She double-checked all her facts and built a case made of unimpeachable data. Tomorrow's edition of the newspaper was going to be a doozy.

Chapter 16

Amanda spent the next morning scraping paint off the elaborate gingerbread-style trim at the back of the Inn. She didn't like being up too high on the ladder, but she was saving her renovation budget for things that she couldn't do herself, and even though scraping paint was tedious it was definitely something she could handle alone. The only good thing about being up the tall ladder was the amazing view. If she turned her head a bit there was an amazing panorama of the beach below, and when the soft wind swirled just right, she could actually hear some of the far off breakers.

Scrubbing the peeling paint off the wood with a wire brush, she heard someone talking below her. Craning her head, Amanda could see the pretty blonde girl who had been visiting her Russian neighbor the other day. The girl was smiling at her, a basket looped over one arm, obviously waiting.

"Hello! I'm Jennifer Peetman. I don't think we've met yet."

Amanda smiled back, tucked her brush into her plastic pail, and carefully went down the steps.

"Hi, I'm Amanda." She slid off the canvas work glove and stuck out her hand. The first thing she noticed about Jennifer was her vivid blue eyes, warm and friendly.

"I hope you don't mind me bothering you like this," Jennifer began, "but I was hoping you'd consider letting me buy some of your apples. The lady I visit has been canning applesauce all week, and your Gravensteins are the best around."

"Gravensteins?" Amanda asked.

"Yeah, that's the main type of apple you have. They're great for eating or cooking, and yours haven't been sprayed so that's a real bonus."

"Please, take all you want. They're just going to waste here. I don't even have time to make a pie." *Or anyone to share it with*, she thought, then instantly pushed that thought down. Where had it come from?

"I've actually seen you before, visiting my neighbor. I haven't had a chance to meet her yet," Amanda said as they walked back to the orchard. "What's her name?"

"Mrs. Petrovski," Jennifer hastily answered, turning her head to scan the ground for apples. "She doesn't get outside much at all. She even feeds the local birds off her back porch. There's a spectacular wild rooster that keeps stopping by for free corn."

"She's been feeding Dumb Cluck?" Amanda's face twisted. "I didn't know that. I kinda hate that rooster."

Jennifer looked up, obviously surprised at Amanda's comment. "Hate him? Why?"

"That stupid chicken keeps crowing at the crack of dawn and waking me up! I know it sounds silly but I think he kinda hates me, too. I had no idea why he kept hanging out around here."

"Well, it might be because of all the free corn or it might be because he's been roosting in your chicken coop."

Amanda's face fell. "Oh, you have *got* to be kidding me! He's been sleeping in my henhouse? Free room and board. No wonder he's been staying."

Her guest shrugged, apologetic. "Sorry, I thought you knew." She picked up and discarded a couple of apples. When Amanda pulled a fresh one off the tree she shook her head.

"I don't need the good ones off the tree for applesauce. She...can use the windfalls."

There was an odd catch in her voice, and Amanda suddenly felt like she'd stepped in something that Jennifer didn't want to discuss. It caught Amanda's attention, and she studied the back of the woman next to her, industriously picking up apples off the ground.

"Have you known Mrs. Petrovski for a long time?" she asked, watching her guest bending over and plopping the bright apples in her basket.

"Not too long."

Amanda bent over, too, scooping up apples and checking that they were in good shape before handing three of them to Jennifer. "I'm afraid I don't speak Russian. Would you please let her know that she can come over anytime and get as many apples as she'd like? I don't want her to feel like she has to run off if I come outside."

"Thank you. I will," Jennifer said as she straightened up, stretching out her back.

"So, is Mrs. Petrovski new to Ravenwood Cove?" Amanda knew she was asking a lot of questions, probably too many, but she had the strangest feeling that Jennifer wasn't telling her everything about her Slavic neighbor.

"Yes, she's new here. Doesn't know anyone really and she's very reclusive and shy. Well, I'd better be going and get these apples over to her," Jennifer said, and with a quick wave of her hand she slipped through the same loose fence board that Mrs. Petrovski had used to run away from Amanda the other day.

Definitely something weird there, Amanda thought to herself, and moved the ladder a few feet over. Maybe some time scraping paint would give her some time to help her figure out her mysterious neighbor, even as she tried to ignore the gaping hole in the dirt of her garden, right under her leaning scarecrow.

Chapter 17

It was amazing how just a few days of sunshine and some new tourists could lift an entire town's spirits. When Amanda strolled down the sidewalk of Main Street, threading her way through the brightly-colored pots of flowering plants and outdoor tables with festive tablecloths, every merchant had a broad smile and a friendly greeting for her.

It had already been a good and productive morning. Dropping off her legal documents to Charles, she'd accidentally interrupted him as he was setting up a chessboard on the table by his office window. After she'd given him the paperwork she couldn't resist sitting down and accepting his invitation to a rousing game of chess. They were nearly evenly matched, which seemed to surprise her handsome lawyer, and there had been a lot of laughing and teasing as they battled over the board. At last, Charles emerged as the victor, barely eking out a win and complimentary of Amanda's chess skills. As she was leaving, Amanda made him promise to give her a rematch in the next few weeks, and when she was out on the sidewalk, had waved at him when she saw him smiling at her from his office window. *Definitely a good way to start the day!*

The breeze carried the smell of cooking garlic from the pizzeria, mixed with the welcoming aroma of Mrs. Mason's freshly-baked bread. Up and down the street almost every shop had a new window display or newly-painted door. The bakery had added a pink- and white-striped awning and a brand new candy counter, full of sweets in large glass jars. People smiled and waved, and she heard story after story of happy kids and new customers and who had read the articles and had come to town. The merchants were thrilled with all the new business, and openly wondered how the seashells had gotten planted on the beach. Amanda did her best to listen and to keep her face carefully neutral when they chattered on about the treasure trove found in the sand, and how parents had wandered into their shops, coupon books in hand.

There was even a red OPENING SOON banner strung across the awning in front of Mr. Appleton's long-abandoned shoe repair shop. Amanda couldn't resist peeking inside the big front window to investigate what the new store would be, and grinned at what she saw. There were several brand new bicycles leaning against the back wall, and a huge dragon kite hung in graceful arcs from the ceiling. A couple other colorful kites had been stacked up on the front counter, and Amanda could just make out a pile of trash that had been swept together in the middle of the floor. A bike and kite store! How fun!

True, she'd come downtown to just do some shopping for the Inn and to pick up some basic groceries, but it didn't turn out to be a simple sort of a day. By the time she'd stashed her purchases back in her car and headed to Ivy's to get a snack, she had already spoken to the shop owners about getting together a merchants' association for Ravenwood, and Mrs. Mason had eagerly volunteered the idea that they could have a weekly farmers market in the town square, where merchants and locals could sell their crafts and food. Amanda loved the idea, and as soon as she sat down at a table in the café she pulled out her phone and called to reserve the Grange hall for the night of the meeting. Her ever-present notebook was filled with scribbles and ideas for ways that everyone could promote each other's businesses and help bring in more tourists and cash.

A farmers market! Fancy that. Maybe some of the local people would want to add their own handicrafts and produce from their gardens. Mrs. Mason had already given her the name and phone number of a woman who made beautiful handmade candles, and told her about Mr. Orwin, who carved big wooden carvings using a small chainsaw. The owner of the pizzeria owned an unused portable pizza oven, and seemed excited about the thought of using it to make fresh pizzas at the farmers market.

Maybe her own business was put on indefinite hold, but it felt wonderful to be doing something for the town.

Amanda went down her list and called anyone she thought might be interested in the idea of a market, and by the time she got off the phone she had several enthusiastic promises from people who swore they would be there.

Perhaps this was going to work. Maybe she wouldn't have to confront the mayor after all. Getting the town to come together and support the sudden influx of tourists might just start a tidal wave of growth and tourism that even the formidable mayor could not stop.

Chapter 18

A new day, and a new list of things to do in downtown Ravenwood Cove. By one o'clock she'd talked with most of the merchants she couldn't reach by phone the day before, and she was feeling hopeful and happy. Time for a break.

The lunchtime aromas from the pizzeria smelled delicious, but by now Ivy's Cafe felt almost like home so Amanda decided to stop there for lunch. She hung up her jacket on the lone coat tree, and several people greeted her when she walked to her booth. Ruby made small talk while Amanda glanced over the menu and ordered a slice of the daily dessert special, German chocolate cake. By the time it had arrived and Amanda had dug her fork into the luscious frosting her lawyer, Charles Timmins, had walked in.

"May I sit down?" he asked, his pleasant face expectant. Amanda's fork hovered in mid-air, stacked with gooey icing. "Of course," she said, gesturing to the wooden chair opposite her, and finally taking a bite of her treat.

Amazing. Surely she'd burned enough calories working on the Inn that this wouldn't go straight to her hips, would it?

"Good, isn't it? Ivy's cakes are almost as good as Mrs. Mason's, but don't tell the town's baker I said that."

Amanda nodded, trying to swallow quickly so she could answer him.

"Nice to see you, Charles. Are you just out for lunch or did you want to talk more about my case?"

"Just in town for some groceries, but I was thinking it was about time for us to meet up and talk about how things are going." He flagged down the waitress and ordered some coffee. As soon as she left he dug through the tabletop caddy for a couple of sugar packets and three creamers. "Anything new with your situation that I should know about?"

Amanda wrinkled her nose in disgust. "Not really. The town may be doing better, but I'm still stuck. No word on how Emmett wound up in my backyard, no zoning or license for my Inn to open, and I'm getting really tired of scraping paint for nothing."

He sat back, a mug of fresh coffee in his hand. "I'm so sorry to hear that. Truthfully, this whole thing may take months or years to get fixed."

"And there's nothing we can do legally?" She tried to tamp down the edge of frustration in her voice, but could tell he heard it anyway.

"I'm afraid not." He caught her glancing at her watch, checking the time. "Late for something?"

Amanda smiled, her cake temporarily forgotten. "I've got to eat and run, actually. Some people coming over in a bit to help move furniture and do some interior painting, so I need to head home pretty quick to meet them. If you stop by I'll probably toss you a paintbrush and a pair of work gloves."

"Who's coming by?" His voice was light, but his brown

eyes were serious over the brim of his upturned mug as he took a sip.

"Detective Landon, Roy and his crew, and Lisa."

"James Landon?"

She nodded, surprised at his worried tone.

Her lawyer leaned forward, his eyebrows drawn together in concern. "If I were you, I'd be very careful of the company you keep, Amanda. James Landon has a history with women that precedes him everywhere, and people are already talking nonstop about you in this little town. Your reputation is tied to the reputation of the Inn, and maybe that sounds strange to someone from a big city, but that's how it works here. If we're able to get your business up and running, you'll need all the good opinions you can get. Besides," he leaned forward and dropped his voice—"you can't be too careful these days."

"Careful of what?"

"Well, we know that bad things, deadly things, have happened in this town in the past. I just want to be sure that you're safe and that no one tries to take advantage of your situation."

"I appreciate that, Charles, I really do. I promise I'll be careful." She took another bite of her cake, and added, "If I can't take her to court, I'm not sure what else I can do."

Charles grimaced in sympathy. "Nothing has been done that's illegal, and I hate to admit it, but with the threat of potential lawsuits from Emmett's heirs, you may want to consider some other options."

"What other options?" Her fork hovered in midair, forgotten.

The look he gave her was sympathetic but the words were blunt. "I hate to tell you this, but as your lawyer I need to be factual. With everything you've told me, I don't see how you're going to be able to hold onto the Inn and make it a viable business."

Amanda felt like she'd been stabbed. She didn't have many advocates, and to have her lawyer say she was going to fail hurt more than she'd admit.

"What are you saying, Charles?"

His soft brown eyes were kind, his eyebrows crinkled with concern. "I'm saying that you need to be practical and think about moving on."

"You mean by selling, don't you?" She could feel her lips become a thin, hard line.

"Yes, I do." He sighed sympathetically. "Look, as your lawyer I feel I should advise you as to the perilous situation you're in financially. I don't see a way out of this, and you need to think about how to escape this mess in as good a shape as possible."

There was something about his sympathy that set Amanda's teeth on edge. "And what do you recommend?"

He leaned forward, his voice calm and low, and a hopeful smiling playing around his lips. "I've been approached by someone who is interested in buying the Inn from you, at a very good price."

"What?" Amanda's eyes were wide with disbelief, but he continued.

"It's a solid all-cash offer that will set you up for years, and enable you to get on with your life, wherever you'd want to go. I think you should consider it."

Amanda had a momentary pang at the sudden thought of leaving Ravenwood Cove. She hadn't had an easy time here, true, but she was starting to really love the small town. Maybe it was the way she'd been able to help somewhat, maybe it was some of the friends she was making, but whatever it was, the thought of leaving definitely hurt.

"And they came to you so you'd present the offer to me? Who was it, anyway?" She had to ask, even though she had a very good idea who'd made the offer.

"Due to attorney-client privilege, I am unable to disclose that information."

Her mouth actually fell open at Charles' statement. "You can't tell me who's offering me cash to sell my inheritance and get outta town?"

Charles shook his head emphatically. "I can't. The offer would be made through a holding company so the party could remain anonymous. I can assure you, though,"—he continued quickly--"that the offer is extremely generous."

"So this mystery person or company is your client, too?"

Charles nodded, waiting.

There was the space of one heartbeat, then two, and Amanda finally said what was on her mind.

"Charles, you're fired."

It was Charles' turn to look stunned, but Amanda was beyond caring. "For you to take them on as a client when you're under retainer to me is a terrible breach of trust. I don't want you as my lawyer anymore, Charles."

"Look, I can tell you're upset, and we can talk later, Amanda. You can have some time to think about things," he stammered quickly, but Amanda was done.

"Time for you to go, Charles." There was a soft chime of a cellphone and Charles answered the call. He nodded and said "okay" a couple of times, then hung up the phone.

Setting down a five-dollar bill to pay for his coffee, he stood and pulled on his coat.

"Charles, there's just one more thing." Amanda could feel the anger simmering just under the surface, and did her best to remain calm.

"Yes?"

"I want my dollar bill back."

Even though he seemed embarrassed and almost apologetic, he dug into his wallet again and pulled out a lone dollar, placing it gently on the tabletop.

"I'm sorry, Amanda, I truly am, but I only want what's best for you. Look, I need to be in my office for an important phone call in the next few minutes. I'll touch base with you again in a couple of days to see how you're doing, and we can talk again," he said, wisely not shaking her hand before heading outside. Through the front window she saw him hurrying away down the street, under a darkening sky.

Rainclouds coming.

Chapter 19

All the way home, her conversation with Charles rolled around in her mind. Someone had actually approached the only lawyer in town to make an anonymous offer to buy the Inn.

If they'd been able to do that, they must've been able to pay a much bigger fee than she could, she was guessing. She thought about Charles' returned dollar bill, crumpled up in her purse.

Gonna burn it, she thought. *Good riddance to bad rubbish.*

By the time she pulled into the circular driveway at the Inn, there was also a car parked there.

A police car. A very familiar looking sheriff deputy's car, to be exact.

Amanda took a deep breath and popped the back hatch open, but as soon as she was out of the car and had taken three steps there was a very familiar figure standing by her rear bumper. She smiled and greeted James as he helped pull out the bags and flowerpots and paint cans that she'd bought.

Well, almost bought. Mrs. Mason had sent the box of macadamia nut cookies over as a thank you and wouldn't take no for an answer, even when Amanda tried to pay.

"Looks like you've been busy."

Amanda balanced the bakery box on one arm while she grabbed the last two grocery bags, and James clicked the hatch shut.

"Yes, lots of errands today. An inn owner's work is never done, you know. You're early."

She glanced sideways at him, only to see him grinning broadly at her, his dark eyes glancing over her outfit with approval. She'd grabbed a simple dress and flat sandals when she'd left the house, perfect for a day that had started out warm and beautiful.

James seemed to realize she had seen his reaction. "Nice to see a lady in a dress once in a while. Most of the girls around here just wear jeans all the time."

Maybe it was her encounter with Charles, maybe it was the appreciative way he was looking her over, or maybe it was the fact that she was standing next to this large man who was looking at her like….like she was a woman.

All of those things made Amanda's alarm bells go off.

No more men, especially charming men with bad reputations. Even if they did have crisp dark hair and smell like leather and the outdoors.

"Only thing I had that was clean today. I'm having some trouble with my washer."

He took the box of cookies from her while she unlocked the front door and pushed the heavy wooden door inward.

"I can take a look at it for you. I'm pretty handy at fixing things. Something was always breaking or falling apart on the farm, and usually I was the lucky one who got assigned to repair detail."

"Farm?"

"My folks have a good-sized horse ranch, about five minutes back toward Highway 101, past Likely. Great place to grow up. You ever ridden a horse before?"

Amanda thought about all the years she'd spent in LA. She'd hardly ever seen a horse, and the thought of being on something that big kind of scared her.

"Not really. Always thought I'd like to try it, though." Perhaps it was a bit of a fib, but she wished it wasn't.

He smiled at her. "I'm sure we can make that happen."

There was a flash of movement and a dark orange blur of determined fur ran past Amanda into the kitchen. James looked up, surprised.

"New friend?"

She laughed and followed the huge cat, setting her bags down on the kitchen counter. It was apparent her furry guest had food on his mind when he started to purr and rub against her bare legs, looking up at her in sad appeal.

"You figured out where the tuna is, didn't ya?" she asked, reaching over to pet the new houseguest. Sighing in resignation, she got a bowl out of the cupboard and headed to the pantry.

"I didn't know you had a cat."

"I don't. Well, I mean I didn't. He kind of showed up here and I guess he decided to stay."

James leaned over and scratched the happy kitty under the chin. "He knows a softie when he sees one."

Tuna plopped in bowl, a full bowl on the floor by the door to the back porch, and Amanda's happy cat was purring contentedly while gulping down the fish.

"What's his name? It's a boy, isn't it?"

Amanda started putting away the groceries, juggling several cans at a time. "I've never looked and he's never told me. Guess he doesn't have a name yet."

James squinted at the cat, his fingers stroking his own chin in mock deep thought. "How about Oscar? Seems to fit him."

"Why Oscar?"

"I had an Uncle Oscar once, and he was a man who always knew what he wanted, just like this little guy."

"Not so little. I'm gonna have to get some regular cat food or he's gonna wipe out my stock of tuna."

James laughed, agreeing, and dug into one of the grocery bags. "I don't know where anything goes," he explained as he started pulling out the food and handing the cans and boxes to her.

He was standing too close, his long frame leaning against the counter as he helped with the food. He'd obviously come dressed to work, wearing an old plaid flannel shirt and faded jeans, with a pair of tennis shoes that had certainly seen better days.

Dressed to clean my place and still looks like he's a model who stepped out of a Wrangler ad, she thought.

Amanda tried to edge away and not look at the tall detective. Somehow just him being in her kitchen was making it feel smaller, almost as though he was dangerous somehow. It made her uncomfortable but she tried to hide it as she rolled the empty grocery bags together and stashed them in the pantry.

"I'd appreciate any help you could give me with that washer. I really don't want to use the laundromat in town." Ages ago she'd had to use the laundromat in the basement of her condo building, and she had memories of a dimly-lit concrete block room with rolls of lint on the floor. After her underwear had mysteriously disappeared out of her unattended dryer she'd done her best to not go back.

"I have some news for you. The final autopsy results came back about Emmett."

It almost felt as if the breath had been pushed out of her. Here it came.

"What...what were the results?"

James seemed almost apologetic. "No cause of death found."

"Are you sure? How can that be?" The edge in her voice was unintentional but she couldn't help it.

"Read it for yourself," James said, and slid over a folded sheaf of papers he'd had tucked in his back pocket.

Amanda frantically scanned the sheet. Emmet Johnson, age…birthplace…skeletal…

The details were black and white, and there wasn't much that she didn't already know. The investigator had listed the boot tips and signet ring found with the body, the clear plastic that had wrapped around it, and the proprietary wrapping tape that had closed the plastic tightly. Amanda tried not to look at the digital photos that had been included in the packet of info. The only new item that Amanda discovered was that the investigator had found an unusual substance in the victim's hair and mouth, listing it as wheat.

She was having trouble reading the extensive technical notes that had been included. Too much medical and legal jargon.

"What's saponification?"

James grimaced. "Trust me, you don't want to know."

She shuddered. "Okay, I'll believe you on that one."

"Probably best," he agreed. "Let's change the subject. When do you want to get to work cleaning?"

A loud knock on the front door startled Amanda a bit. She smiled at James, setting down the folded report on the kitchen island. "Perfect timing."

Perfect timing to not have to talk about bodies and plastic and reality. And, she admitted, perfect timing to not be alone with the handsome detective, James Landon.

Oscar, newly-named and full of tuna, trotted alongside her as she opened the door. Lisa and Roy and two of Roy's crew, John and Nathan, were standing there. Lisa's eyes were instantly drawn to the huge cat.

"New friend?"

***

Amanda got changed into her work clothes, complete with a bandana to cover her hair and a protective dust mask, and went back to the kitchen to give her small crew instructions. They spent the rest of the afternoon moving furniture, taking down long curtains crusted with years of dust, and rolling up the oriental carpets so they could be moved outside and the dirt beat out of them. The whole team moved room by room through the Inn, starting on the ground floor. Roy and James seemed to be doing most of the heavy lifting, but everyone pitched in where they could, and there was a lot of joking and laughter as they methodically cleaned everything.

By the time they'd moved upstairs, Amanda headed back to the kitchen to make a fresh pitcher of lemonade and put some cookies on a tray. Oscar tagged along with her, following close by her heels wherever she went. As Amanda opened the freezer to get some ice she could hear the thumping and scraping sounds overhead. The crew was moving the antique bedroom furniture away from the walls and everything was being wiped down and vacuumed. No more dust bunnies, no more cobwebs. Even if she couldn't open the Inn, just getting things clean and in order made her feel a bit better about things.

And, if a miracle happened, she'd be as ready as possible for new guests.

Balancing a tray with pitcher and pastries, she headed back up, Oscar right with her, rubbing against her ankles in a constant bid for attention.

"Nothing on this tray for you, buddy," she said, winking at the cat.

He sat down at the top of the stairs, apparently unconcerned, and started licking his front paw.

"Looks like I've got a new housemate."

***

Lisa and Roy teamed up, and the two crew members took over a different bedroom, while James and Amanda worked on a third. It was a lovely guest room, and Amanda was happy to open the French doors leading to the balcony, letting in the cool sea breeze. The ocean was dappled green and blue today, reflecting the sunlight shining through the few white clouds slowly rolling by.

"Seems so peaceful up here," she sighed. "Sometimes I forget just how much has happened recently in my life, or how many people want this Inn to fail."

James set down the walnut nightstand. "You mean the mayor." It wasn't a question.

"Yes, and all the people who won't stand up to her. I've never wanted anything in my life so much as to fit in here and build a life, and it feels like I'm getting stopped at every turn." Amanda turned her face away, pretending to be wiping down the wainscoting so James couldn't see the raw emotion in her eyes.

"I'm sorry, Amanda. Really I am." His voice was warm, but Amanda knew if she gave in to his sympathy she'd probably just start to bawl outright.

"That old bat. You know, I've never really thought of the idea of having an enemy, but that is exactly what Mrs. Sandford is to me. My enemy. It's like she's deliberately trying to shut out every bit of hope and light and money that I can have in my life, and I just can't stand to be around her."

James was silent, waiting, as she went on. "She's one of those enemies that the Reverend would say I should be praying for. Apparently, I'm really bad at that."

He shrugged. "It's hard to forgive when you feel someone's out to get you."

"I just want to smack her disapproving face. Every time I see her that's what I picture. WHACK. With a fish. A big slimy one."

He burst out laughing and she couldn't help but giggle. The thought of the mayor being cracked across the face with a limp cod was too funny for words.

"She wasn't always like that, you know. People don't just become cranky and stuck in their ways for no reason, all good or all bad."

"What are you trying to say?"

He sighed. "Look, she gets on my nerves, too, but I grew up here. I know that years ago she used to be the belle of the town around here. It wasn't until after she was married and her first baby died that she started to change. Her husband wasn't an easy man, and I think her prestige and wealth she'd had as a girl kind of dried up."

"Maybe she dried up, too." Amanda didn't want to feel sympathy for the mayor, and it showed.

"Maybe. It's hard to be in one place your whole life, where everyone knows everyone and is in your business. It makes you worry about what people think about who you married, or if your new house you bought is less expensive than the last one you bought, or that your husband may have a roving eye."

Amanda felt a sudden twinge of sympathy, and ruthlessly tried to quell it. She really didn't want to feel it for the mayor at all.

"Doesn't excuse her bad behavior, I know, but thought it would help for you to hear a bit about her. My Dad says she used to be really well-liked in town. She didn't always push people around like this."

Amanda thought about that, trying to imagine the mayor as a carefree bride, hopeful for her future. It wasn't easy.

She needed some time to think about it. Maybe the mayor changed because she thought she had to change, or because she was afraid what would happen to her world if she didn't. Maybe she was just trying to survive.

Amanda subdued any twinges of compassion as she furiously cleaned in the corner between the wall and the massive bed. *Yes, people change,* she thought, *but that doesn't give anyone the right to treat other people like garbage. Just because she had a bad life doesn't mean she can act like she rules everyone else.*

She saw the corner of the torn envelope the moment she flipped back the corner of the rug. She picked it up and was just going to toss it into the small garbage can she was dragging with her through the room, when her eyes caught some writing on the outside.

YOU HAVE TWO HOURS

Big dark letters, written in an angry scrawl across the front.

Amanda's blood ran cold. This wasn't a piece of mail carelessly left. This was something that had been deliberately hidden, and that was much more personal and angry.

She glanced sideways at James, who was busy ripping down the heavy velvet curtains, a cloud of dust poofing around his head.

It took only a moment for Amanda to fold the envelope in half and stuff it into her pocket. She patted it hard to ensure there'd be no telltale bulge, and pulled the corner of the rug back to see if there was anything else there.

Nothing.

She'd have to read it later, when she was by herself. As she kept working she had a twinge of guilt about not sharing it with the hard-working detective, now climbing the stepstool to clean out the hanging light fixture. It wasn't that she thought he was working against her. It was just that it felt almost like family business, this murder and this letter.

Family business. If there were incriminating things in that piece of paper stuffed into her pocket she would tell him. She just wanted to see what it said first.

Chapter 20

By late afternoon they were all tired and covered in dust. Amanda could see the fatigue in their movements and when the crew moved toward the staircase to the third floor, she made a quick decision.

"Let's call it a day." She was exhausted, and had been itching to get some time to herself so she could read the letter she'd discovered.

James looked at her, not surprised. "Amanda, are you trying to be nice to us, or are you trying to keep us away from master suite?"

The words were so plain and open they hurt. "Maybe both."

Roy and his crew may not have understood why Amanda wouldn't want them seeing the suite, but they nodded and headed downstairs, trailed by Lisa.

James wasn't so easily dissuaded. "You sure you don't want help with that room?"

She looked at him, assessing. Maybe he meant well, but he was still a detective investigating a murder.

"No, thanks. I'd like to work on it by myself. There are some fragile things in there that I really should box up and I'd like to take my time."

He nodded, understanding both her excuse and her reasoning. "How about I go take a look at that washer for you?"

"That would be great. It's in the laundry room off the kitchen."

He loped downstairs toward the kitchen, and she could hear him rummaging around in her tool drawer, slamming it shut before she heard the floor squeak by the laundry room.

Now. She needed a place to read the letter, alone.

It took only moments for her to quietly head upstairs and click the door shut behind her in the still-cluttered master suite. She sat down on the dusty bed, took a deep breath, and eased the crinkly envelope out of her pocket, smoothing it open.

The paper was dry and almost brittle with age as she unfolded it. She could feel the adrenaline starting to course through her veins as she read the first line.

My patience has come to an end.

Oh, no. She kept reading, her eyes raking over the horrible words, taking it in like she'd take in desperate gulps of bad air.

If you know what's good for you you'll leave tonight. We've had enough history you know I can make you disappear, and I've got enough connections that you know I can get away with it. If you aren't gone by dawn I'll rip everything you love away from you and you'll never even see me coming. You have until midnight.

Her hands were shaking as she reread the threatening letter. Was it from her uncle, or from the killer? Why would someone want to send someone out of state?

It took her almost ten minutes to dig through the paperwork that her uncle had left behind, frantically scanning long-discarded mail and notes jotted on scraps of paper before she found what she was looking for.

It was a love letter her uncle had written to her aunt, stashed with a shoebox full of keepsakes, probably from the time they'd been dating. They'd left it behind, another sad testament to how fast they had fled, and what parts of their life they'd had to abandon.

She smoothed out the two letters and laid them side by side on the bed.

The writing was totally different. Whoever had written the mysterious letter had not been her uncle. Whoever wrote this letter was threatening to murder him.

That meant two things. Someone had been threatening her family and that was why they had fled and never returned, and her uncle hadn't been the killer.

Her thoughts flashed instantly to her dead uncle and aunt, with almost a feeling of embarrassment that she'd ever suspected either of them in the first place. Whatever they had been, they weren't murderers.

Now she just had to figure out who wrote the message, and why.

She picked up both letters and headed downstairs to the laundry room. Time to get James and the sheriff's department involved.

Chapter 21

When Amanda found the old bicycle in the back of the chicken coop, she wasn't sure if it was junk or treasure. She brushed off the straw and cobwebs, then wheeled it up to the back of the Inn, by the hose and spigot. Even though the front tire was flat and there was a lot of loud squeaking when she rolled it, Amanda could tell that this bike was a classic from decades ago. With bright red fenders and a broad wicker basket over the front wheel, it would be perfect for runs into town on errands. Truth was, she didn't always need her car, and it would be nice to have something that gave her some exercise and didn't burn up gas.

And, at the rate she was spending money to get the Inn repaired she couldn't afford the extra expense of gas, anyway.

She dug out a soft brush and some old towels, and got to work. Within half an hour it gleamed, water droplets still running down the bright paint and pooling on the brick patio. A bit of three-in-one oil and adjustment of the brakes and it almost looked brand new. Amanda rummaged around in the shed and discovered an old pump, and after a bit of wrangling with it she was able to get the flat tire inflated.

Perfect! For some reason, just looking at the bike, gleaming with glossy lipstick-red paint and bright chrome, made her happy

She'd already printed out the fliers announcing the first meeting of the new Merchant and Farmers Market

Association, so it took only minutes for Amanda to change into clean jeans and a fresh blouse and to pedal her way toward town.

The soft breeze tasted a bit of salt and was cool on her face as she coasted downhill, loving the crispness of the autumn air. *Going to be tough going back up*, she thought, *but I could definitely use the exercise.*

Amanda took the time to go into every shop on Main Street, and the merchants greeted her as if she were an old friend. They seemed excited and hopeful about the upcoming meeting and told her tale after tale about how their business was suddenly booming.

The only problem was at Petrie's general store. Brian Petrie was staffing the counter, ringing up a new garden rake for Mr. Henderson, but when he saw Amanda he motioned at her as if he wanted to be sure she'd come over to talk to him.

Amanda put on her best smile and pulled a flyer off the stack in her hand. As soon as Mr. Henderson had left with his slug bait and new rake, Brian pointed an accusatory finger at Amanda, mock anger on his face.

"I think you're avoiding me, little lady. Every time I see you on the street you're talking to one of the other store owners and you haven't said two words to me in the past couple of weeks. What's up? Did I sell you a garden hose that leaked or something?"

She laughed, and then she lied. "No, no, nothing like that. I've just been so busy that I haven't had a chance to really swing by and talk much." She didn't tell him that she'd waited until she was sure Sally, the assistant manager, was there at the same time Brian was. She definitely didn't feel comfortable being alone with him. She kept thinking about what the medical examiner had found with the body in her garden.

Brian looked skeptical at her explanation. "Okay, so you're not mad at me, then?"

Amanda grinned and lied again. "Of course not!"

Before she left, she stopped by the woodstove benches so she could say hello to Mrs. Granger, then stepped out into the crisp air of Main Street. She gulped it as if she'd been holding her breath the whole time she'd been inside the store, then clutched her file of papers and headed over to the next shop.

By the time Amanda had handed out most of the flyers it was time for breakfast. *Maybe a warm cinnamon roll at Cuppa*, she thought, happy to turn her new bike toward her favorite little coffee shop.

Tory Sherwood, the owner, was busy rolling out dough in the back room when Amanda walked in. Her friend Meg was bent over, putting a tray of fresh scones in the pastry display case. At the cheerful sound of the bell over the door, she straightened up with a smile and wiped her hands on her white apron.

"Hey! I was just going to call you. I wanted to make sure to invite you to my grandmother's birthday party," Meg said.

"Mrs. Granger's birthday party? When is it?"

"This Saturday at six, in the back meeting room at Ivy's. Gram would love to see you. You're one of the few people that she really likes around here."

138

Amanda laughed. "I can't imagine why. Maybe she just doesn't know me too well yet, I guess. What can I bring?"

"Just bring something for the potluck," Meg said. "She's got enough stuff already. At ninety years old you tend to accumulate a lot of things. Oh, and don't tell her about it. It's a surprise party."

Amanda grinned. "I'll be there with bells on."

Chapter 22

Pedaling up the hill wasn't nearly as much fun as coasting down into town, but Amanda consoled herself with the idea that it was free exercise and that her bike basket was full of fresh goodies for dinner. She was also happily musing over how well things were going for the merchants, and trying to think of new ways to help the town. By the time she rolled onto the gravel drive at the front of the Inn she was panting a bit from exertion, and ready for something to drink and maybe a nap.

It was never going to happen. There were three vehicles parked in front of her beautiful Inn; two cars and a van. She hopped off the bike and rolled it toward the front door where four men stood, obviously waiting.

"Are you Mrs. Graham?"

"Not Mrs., but I'm Amanda Graham. What can I do for you gentlemen?"

The man was short and round, wearing dark coveralls. He seemed almost embarrassed as he handed Amanda an official-looking sheet of paper.

"Pest inspection. The city's been getting some complaints that the Ravenwood Inn may have rats, which are infesting the neighborhood."

"Rats! What are you talking about? I've never had a rat problem here." She scanned the document, her mind flashing to the evidence of mice she'd discovered in the kitchen. Definitely not *rats*.

She looked up, her gaze raking over the quiet men. "Are you all here for rats?"

A guy in an orange t-shirt and jeans stepped forward, holding out another sheet of paper. "Sewer inspection. There've been some reports of bad smells from your place and I've been told–"

"You've been told to come check it out. Let me guess. *All* of you have been told to come check problems at the Inn, right?" They nodded, and when the next man stepped forward, Amanda instantly recognized him. It was the terse building inspector who'd looked through the Inn when she first moved to Ravenwood.

"What are you doing here? You've already gone over the Inn with a fine-toothed comb, and you know what condition it was in."

"Heard you've been doing a bunch of work out here and haven't pulled any permits, Miss Graham. That's a serious violation and you know I have to investigate that whenever we get a report—"

Her temper boiled over as she interrupted him. "Get a report. Right! Did any of you geniuses figure out that if you *all* get reports at the same time maybe someone is just out to get me? Maybe someone is trying to harass and intimidate me?"

The building inspector seemed surprised. "Um, we don't know anything about that. We just do what we're told. Any time there's a complaint we have to investigate and report back to the city."

"To the city or to the city *council*?" There was that headache again, right between her eyes.

"To the city."

"And just who, do you suppose, filed all these complaints about me?"

He shifted nervously from foot to foot. "We're not allowed to say. It's kept anonymous."

Amanda could feel her blood pressure rise. "Anonymous, huh?" She'd begun to hate that word. "We'll just see about *that*."

Trying to keep her temper under control was a challenge as the apologetic workmen started going through her precious Inn, armed with flashlights and clipboards. They poked in every corner, even going into the untouched attic to check for violations or permit issues. The rat guy (for that's what Amanda had termed him in her mind) walked around the perimeter of the Inn, then the entire property, poking a long stick into holes and examining the wooden siding for chew marks. Amanda made sure they were doing what they said they would and once she was satisfied that they were, she grabbed her purse and headed for her car.

It took only minutes to drive down into town, park the car, and stomp into the city hall. Painted white with some brick on the façade, the building was easy to find, right on the main town square by the tall flagpole. The bespectacled clerk at the desk looked surprised, then alarmed, as Amanda stormed past the counter and toward the open door on the mayor's office.

"You, you can't go in there!" he was sputtering, just as Amanda stepped onto the Persian carpet and glared at the mayor.

"You won't get away with this! I don't care how long it takes, but I'm going to be sure that justice is done and that you won't be able to pick on the citizens of Ravenwood ever again! You have no right to persecute me –"

The mayor suddenly stood and cut her off. "Miss Graham, I have no idea what you're babbling about."

Amanda could see a few people drifting out of their offices to check what the commotion was, and she tried to keep her voice a bit lower, even though it was shaking with fury.

"How *dare* you! How dare you single me out for your vindictive, petty issues! You may have backed me into a corner, but don't be surprised when I come out fighting. I don't care how many inspectors you throw at me. You haven't beaten me yet!"

"Young lady, you are completely hysterical." The mayor's voice was calm, but the expression on her face was finally beginning to reflect alarm.

Amanda took a deep breath, trying to restrain herself from just leaping across the desk and strangling the old bat. "I don't care how miserable your life has been. You have no right to take it out on honest citizens who are just trying to make a living." There was a rustle behind her and as she turned her heart fell.

James was standing there, looking at her, his eyebrows raised in casual surprise.

"Are you done now?" he asked, arms crossed over his chest.

"Just about," she answered, and then turned to the mayor and stuck out her tongue. It was juvenile, it was ineffective, but she wasn't much at swearing and giving the mayor the finger just wasn't her style.

James gently put a large hand around the upper part of Amanda's arm and turned her toward the door, quietly chuckling to himself. *Spitfire!*

As he escorted her outside, Amanda tried to take a few deep breaths to slow her heart rate and get herself under control. By the time James had gestured to a wooden bench under a nearby shade tree, the adrenaline she'd been using for anger had turned to shaking. She wasn't used to yelling like that or confronting anyone, and she still wasn't sure if it felt good or not.

James plopped down on the bench beside her and they silently surveyed the green of the town square for a few moments. A few people were picnicking at the tables near the small playground, but otherwise it was mostly deserted.

"Having an exciting day, are we?"

Amanda snorted in disgust. "She started it."

"What happened?"

It hurt to have to even say the words, how she'd been targeted for the mayor's vendetta. "I came back home today to find all sorts of inspectors and workmen who want to crawl over every inch of my Inn. They said they'd been tipped off that, oh"--she started to tick off the items on her fingers--"I have rats, I have been building without a permit, and have sewer issues that are grossing out my neighbors." She slumped back on the bench. "It seems like every time I start to make some headway in this town I'm getting smacked back down, and I've had it!"

"And you're sure it was the mayor?"

"Who else? She's out to get me. I'd keep fighting but at this point I don't even know where to turn next."

"You've got friends here, Amanda." James' voice was calm and sincere. "You've got people who want to help you, and we're doing the best we can. Just so you know, I turned the letters over as evidence in your case, and the lab techs are having a field day testing them."

"Anything?"

"Nothing conclusive. No prints, but they're working on the handwriting. The good news is that it looks like we'll be able to rule out your uncle. I compared those two letters and agree with you. The handwriting is totally different." James was quiet, thoughtful. "I'm working as hard as I can on an official level to solve Emmett's murder, but there may be places you can go and things you can ask that I just can't as a detective."

Amanda turned toward him, surprised. "What do you mean?"

"I think that the only way we can make sure you stay and are happy here in town is to solve Emmett's murder, Amanda. Look, I'll keep you posted on what's going on about the investigation. The matter with the mayor is completely separate." He sighed, sounding tired. "If you're being harassed, you may need to get your lawyer involved."

"I fired him."

James looked surprised but didn't ask any questions. "Well, you may need a different one, then."

Amanda thought about his statement. Even though she agreed with the idea, the reality of having to pay a lawyer's fee was sobering.

Apparently James could read the hesitation in her eyes. "I'd also recommend you don't let people know that your uncle probably wasn't involved in the murder. The less people know, the more chance there is for someone to slip up and reveal themselves. There are layers of deceit and old lies built up around this, and you've become the victim of them all. I don't want you to be hurt and frankly, I'd like you to stay."

Amanda looked up, surprised, to find James smiling at her. "You know, it isn't every day that I meet someone who'll let me help them bury about a hundred seashells on a freezing cold beach before daylight. That type of girl is kinda rare. Almost worth getting my feet wet."

She laughed and stood up, smoothing imaginary crumbs off her pants, ready to go.

"Next time, wear your boots."

Chapter 23

"I brought you some doughnut holes, Mrs. Granger."

The old lady put her hand out for the box, smacking her lips together with glee. "One of my favorites! You shouldn't have." From the grip she had on the box, Amanda knew she *should* have.

"I left my teeth in a glass on the kitchen windowsill. Can you get them for me, dear?"

That was a first. Amanda dutifully got the cup of water, teeth included, and Mrs. Granger expertly popped them into her mouth.

"Makes eating them doughnut holes much easier, doncha know," she said, matter-of-factly, taking a big bite with evident relish. "How did you know I was at home?"

"I stopped by Cuppa this morning, and Meg told me."

The old lady nodded her head. "So, what's new about Emmett? I hear they figured out it was him."

"Yes, they did. I'm kind of glad things are calming down a bit, even if I'm still not able to have guests at the Inn." Amanda dug a chocolate doughnut hole out of the offered box.

"You've been getting out at all these days?" Mrs. Granger asked.

Amanda nodded, enjoying watching the old lady gobble down the pastries. "A bit. I've been talking to some of the townspeople about everything that's been going on."

"Anyone 'fessed up to leaving all those big seashells down on the beach yet?"

Amanda kept her eyes on the pastry box. "Not yet."

"Uh HUH." From the skeptical tone of Mrs. Granger's voice, Amanda knew instantly that the old lady had an inkling of who might be behind the exotic discoveries, and maybe even the mysterious boom of tourism in town.

"How about anyone 'fessing up to planting Emmett in your garden?"

"No one's come forward, but let's just say I have my suspicions." Amanda tried to keep from sounding bitter.

The old lady leaned forward, all ears. "Really? Do tell!"

Amanda wasn't sure what made her hesitate, except that the phrase 'innocent until proven guilty' kept rolling around in her head.

"I need to check out a few things first, Mrs. Granger, okay? I promise I'll tell you as soon as I know more."

The old lady sat back, obviously disappointed. "Well, *pooh*. Was hoping that all this stuff you were doing around town woulda brought you some new info."

She waited, seemingly hoping that Amanda would crack and tell her some news, but when the young woman didn't she sighed deeply and took a bite out of one of the doughnut holes.

"So, I figure you're here to get information about as much as you're here to bring me baked goods." Amanda tried to ignore the occasional crumb that Mrs. Granger would eject from her mouth.

Amanda did her best to look uninterested, and asked, "Tell me about Brian Petrie and Emmett. Did they get along?"

The little lady snorted. "Not a snowball's chance in hell of those two ever having gotten along. They used to fight like cats and dogs, even in elementary school. Brian's a good kid, even if he does blow off those illegal fireworks on the Fourth of July. Always sounds like a damn war zone by his house."

Amanda knew that she had to keep the conversation on track or Mrs. Granger would be telling her all sorts of weird details about townspeople she probably really didn't want to know.

"So they fought?"

The old lady snorted, waving a doughnut hole at Amanda for emphasis. "You should've seen the fist fight they had about ten years ago. It was epic."

Amanda perked up. "Fight? What was it about?"

"Who knows why men fight? All I know is that I was standing in line to buy my movie ticket for the Sound of Music sing-along, and then Brian Petrie comes storming in, shouting something about Emmett being a rat bastard, and punched him dead in the face. Caught him a good one." She mimicked a poking fist. "Flipped him butt over teakettle across the concession counter and right into the popcorn machine. Broke the doors on the front of it and popcorn went flying everywhere."

Amanda leaned in, expectant. "And then what happened?"

"I never did get my popcorn that night." Mrs. Granger stuck out her bottom lip, actually sulking. "And they have real butter on their popcorn; not that cheap crap at the multiplex."

Amanda tried to keep her voice calm. "I mean, what happened to the two men who were fighting?"

"Oh, that. Well, Brian wound up in jail for a day or so, but they let him out. I don't know if the charges were thrown out or what, but that's all I remember." Mrs. Granger popped another doughnut hole in her mouth, happy again.

Time to change the subject, Amanda thought. "I got to meet Jennifer Peetman the other day. Seems like a nice girl."

Mrs. Granger took a swig of milk. "She's a peach. Used to run the local canned food drive every year she was in high school. Worst piano player I ever heard. Too bad about last year, though."

"Oh, did something happen to her while she was off at college?"

Mrs. Granger looked surprised, white crumbs of doughnut glaze scattered around her lips.

"Jennifer never went to college. I mean about the baby she gave up for adoption."

"What baby?"

"Her baby. She had to do it all by herself, since her folks aren't in the picture and God knows that the father wasn't going to lift a finger to help her."

Amanda was confused, and her face showed it. "I thought she was at college for the past couple of years, learning Russian? That's what she told me the other day, why she's able to talk to my neighbor, the Russian lady."

"Well, I can understand why she wouldn't want her personal business out on everyone's lips but I *never* gossip so her secret is safe with me." The old lady shifted in her seat and leaned closer to Amanda, dropping her voice to a near-whisper. "She went off to her aunt's house in Portland and had the baby there. After a while she moved back here to Ravenwood Cove, and then that Russian lady moved in. What's her name? Mrs. Vodka?"

"Mrs. Petrovski," Amanda answered automatically, her mind whirling. Either Jennifer had flat out lied to her, or Mrs. Granger was wrong. Amanda weighed the possibilities. It was true the Mrs. Granger had probably been born about a thousand years ago, but she certainly valued knowing what was going on in people's personal lives the way some women valued diamonds and fabulous shoes. She might have confused about who had gone to Portland to have a baby, but somehow that didn't seem too likely.

"I remember the day Frank Petrie went to talk to your Uncle Conrad."

"Who?" Amanda had started to realize that Mrs. Granger's conversations jumped around as much as a toad on a hot skillet.

"Well, Frank Petrie is Brian's older brother. That night Frank went and talked to Conrad, after that loud argument in the diner. Charles had told him about the confrontation when Frank went into Ivy's to get a burger and I guess he was real upset about the whole thing. Frank was new on the police force, years before he moved to Idaho to work at the ski resort up there, and he and Emmett were real good friends. Went to school together, in the same class, doncha know." Amanda leaned forward, rapt and scared to interrupt the little lady in case she'd go off on another tangent.

"Frank always was too aggressive. He got kicked off the football team for being overly rough, and that's saying something in this town. Guess he pulled Conrad over on his way home and gave him quite a piece of his mind about how Conrad had treated his good friend." Mrs. Granger scoffed and took another swig of milk. "Frank always was a jackass."

Amanda's mind was scrambling, trying to go over the new information, when the old lady grinned at her.

"You are coming to my surprise birthday party, aren't you?"

Amanda's mouth opened in shock. "How did you know about that?" She shook a single finger at the old lady in mock anger. "Mrs. Granger, is there *anything* in Ravenwood Cove that you don't know about?"

The old lady sighed and pulled a plastic measuring cup out of her purse. "If I'm so damn smart, how did my reading glasses wind up in the kitchen drawer and I've got this thing in my handbag?"

Chapter 24

Amanda balanced the big bowl of potato salad on her hip as she locked up her car, parked in front of the Liberty Theater. Since Ravenwood Cove had gotten more visitors, parking was definitely tougher than it used to be on Main Street, but today it was even worse since it seemed the entire village had turned out for Mrs. Granger's ninetieth birthday party. Other people up and down the street were getting out of their cars and pulling out goodies to add to the potluck. Amanda could smell the hot bread Mrs. Mason had in her basket before she even got to the door, and knew that Meg had insisted on making the huge birthday cake herself.

The little restaurant was more packed than usual for a Saturday night, with folks chatting and greeting each other in the main room and long tables set together in the back meeting room for all the dishes people were setting out. The café's back room was usually reserved for weekly meetings of the Elks or the boy scouts, but today it was lovely to see how many people cared for Mrs. Granger. The ninety-year-old birthday girl was ensconced in an upholstered chair, probably brought in just for this occasion, and was animatedly talking with a group of people clustered around her.

Hope I'm that loved when I turn ninety, Amanda thought as she set her homemade potato salad on the buffet and waved at Grace TwoHorses. George Ortiz and Charles Timmins were discussing the finer points of barbecuing beef brisket, and Thomas Fox was chatting about dahlias with one of the Hortman brothers. Amanda still couldn't tell the brothers apart; they were so similar.

Mayor Sandford had apparently brought two whole smoked salmon for the party. *Only the best to impress*, Amanda thought as she ducked into the other room. It was difficult enough to be at the same party as the mayor; she certainly didn't need to be in the same vicinity.

Meg was frantically gesturing at her from the restaurant's kitchen, so Amanda pushed her way through the swinging door to find out why her friend looked so upset.

"She wants all the candles on her cake. All ninety!" Meg exclaimed, pointing to the big sheet cake on the Formica counter. She'd decorated it with pink and purple swirls and lettering, her grandmother's favorite colors. "How am I going to put ninety little candles on this cake, get them all lit, and keep them going at the same time?"

Amanda suppressed a laugh but tried to be helpful. "Can you just set the thing on fire?" she asked, trying to keep a straight face.

"Ha ha freakin' HA. Very funny, 'Manda. Just for that, you get to help light them all." She waved off Amanda's mock protest. "Too late. You volunteered."

Amanda glanced through the service window that looked out into the main room. "Lots of people here today. Maybe I can just stay in the kitchen with you."

Meg's eyebrows went up. "You're trying to hide in here."

"Maybe. I just have attacks of shyness once in a while. Big gatherings kind of make me nervous."

Time for some tough love. "Oh, no. You get out there and mingle." When Meg saw the hesitation on her friend's face her tone turned gentle. "There are two reasons you need to go out there, Amanda. One: if this is going to be your hometown you need to get used to parties and festivals and stuff like that. We use any excuse we can to get together. Wait until you see the lighting of the Christmas tree in the town square. That gets people coming in from Morganville and Likely and most of the outlying farms."

Amanda sighed. "What's the other reason?"

"No one's been arrested yet for Emmett's death, and I haven't heard anything new for a while. This is a great opportunity to talk to people and find out what they know. They're not going to expect to be questioned at an old lady's birthday party."

Amanda surveyed the crowd. Brian Petrie was just walking in the front door, grinning widely and greeting people, and bearing a huge bouquet of hothouse flowers. Her mind went back to the fact that Emmett's body has been wrapped in plastic and sealed with packing tape from Brian's store. It was true that she was still avoiding talking to Brian as much as possible ever since she found out that gruesome fact, but maybe tonight was a good time to practice her interrogation skills.

If she had any.

"Okay, I'll try."

Meg handed her a full wineglass. "Take this out to Gram, okay? She asked for it twenty minutes ago but I've been so busy back here I haven't had a chance to give it to her."

"Your grandmother drinks wine?" For some reason, the thought of being that old and drinking liquor seemed odd.

Meg chuckled. "She told me once that at her age she was tempted to take up skydiving and smoking cigars. Let's just say that wine is much less worrisome to me."

After Amanda delivered the glass of wine to the chatting guest of honor, George Ortiz announced that the pastor was going to say grace. This surprised Amanda a bit, but she respectfully bowed her head while Pastor Tom said a simple prayer, thanking God for the food and for Mrs. Granger.

After the crowd echoed 'amen' there was a polite but enthusiastic rush for the buffet table and Amanda tried to look casual as she stepped into the back of the line, right beside Brian Petrie. As they shuffled forward toward the potluck dinner she quickly ran over ideas about how to talk to Brian about his relationship with Emmett, and just as quickly discarded them. How in the world was she supposed to interrogate someone over coleslaw and deviled eggs?

The buffet table was nearly sagging from all of the homemade dishes that had been put on its red gingham tablecloth-covered top. Several of the kids were already swarming around the nearby dessert table and were being shooed away occasionally by an unconcerned adult. There was a big space open on the dessert table, just waiting for Mrs. Granger's birthday cake and all of its ninety lit birthday candles.

Meg took one of the crockery plates and followed behind Brian, scooping up food from the various dishes but not really watching what she was putting on her plate.

What do I say to this guy? she frantically wondered. *How do I open the conversation to ask him if he knew his packing tape was used in a murder?*

"So, I guess you've been keeping up with the news from my place," she said loudly to Brian's back, watching him take a huge helping of the smoked salmon.

Brian turned, startled. "Oh, hi, Amanda. Um, yeah. I've been reading about it in the paper. How are you?"

She tried to keep her voice calm and indifferent. "Doing okay. Just kinda of busy with all the police stuff and still trying to get the Inn fixed up." Amanda followed Brian into the main room and took the open seat beside him, balancing her full plate on her lap. He looked kind of startled but scooted over politely so she had plenty of room.

Juggling her dinner on her lap and trying to ask discreet questions at the same time was not going to be easy, but she was going to try. Amana poked at a lone meatball with her fork, then cleared her throat as she tried to think of what to say.

"... So how are things with you?" she asked. Brian hastily swallowed a mouthful of lasagna and nodded at her. "Good, good," he said. "We're doing a big sale on stuff for winterizing your house, so maybe you should stop by. Never too early to get started for bad weather, and you do have the biggest house in town."

"Well, I'm not sure how much I'll need to do that. Right now the Inn is closed and I can't open it to visitors because of the city council restrictions, and because of the murder investigation." She shifted nervously in her chair. "I keep finding out more about the guy who was buried in my garden." She speared a pineapple chunk with her fork, her eyes carefully on her plate. "You didn't happen to know Emmett did you?" she said, trying to sound nonchalant.

Brian swiveled his head toward her, his jaw set in a straight hard line. "Yeah, I knew him," he said. "Everyone in town knew that bastard."

Amanda knew Emmett hadn't been popular, and Brian certainly wasn't trying to give her any other opinion. *Careful, Amanda*, she thought. *Don't blow this.*

"From what I hear, Emmett didn't have a lot of friends in this town. Is that right?"

Brian snorted. "The people who *didn't* want to kill Emmett didn't *know* Emmett," he said. "We went through school together; twelve years of school and he was a weasel from the moment I met him. Did you know he dated my sister for a while? Broke her heart."

Amanda hadn't known that fact.

"Oh, really?" She tried to keep her voice calm. "What happened?"

"Let's just say that Emmett was a complete jerk who couldn't keep his hands to himself, even if he's supposedly engaged to someone. Can't say that I'm sorry he's dead at all," Brian added, turning his whole body to face her. "That guy did things in this town that'd make your blood curdle and I'm glad somebody had the guts to finally do him in. Now, if you'll excuse me, I'm going to go refill my glass," he said, getting up and taking his completely full cup with him.

So much for my interrogation techniques, Amanda thought, morosely looking around the room. A few stragglers were still coming in from time to time and she was surprised to see that James must've arrived when she was in the back kitchen. He had a young man with him, a tall fellow who bore a strong family resemblance and who seemed intent on charming every young lady in the room.

By the time James and Ruby had made sure to turn off the smoke detectors, and the blazing fire of the birthday cake had been brought from the kitchen, James had worked his way around the room to come stand by Amanda. They both joined in the hearty singing, James' strong baritone a nice addition. Mrs. Granger clapped excitedly while everyone sang, her glasses reflecting the near-bonfire set down in front of her. She finally leaned back from the heat of all of the candles. "Well, somebody better help me blow these out! I ain't got the lungs to do it myself, doncha know," she said, pointing a crooked finger at the crowd in the room. There was a general laugh and several people stepped forward to help with the candles, even though George Ortiz was waving a fire extinguisher as a joke.

"Don't make me get the fire chief," he said, finally putting the extinguisher down.

James looked at the huge cake, now smoking from the snuffed out candlewicks. "Sorry I'm late. Had to wrap some things up at work," he said to no one in particular, even though he was shoulder-to-shoulder with Amanda.

"No problem. At least you get cake. Who's the guy with you?"

James followed Amanda's gaze. "Oh, that's my brother Derek. He'd never miss this party for Mrs. Granger. When we were little she was our after school babysitter, until our dad would come pick us up. She was pretty much like a gramma to us, and we still love her."

Amanda tried to picture these two tall, handsome men with dark hair as little boys, eating cookies at Mrs. Granger's house.

"Ever spank you? You look like the sort who would deserve it."

He snorted, amused. "Wouldn't you like to know! Anyway, I'm not the troublemaker. If you wanna talk to a bad boy, that's the guy right over there," he said, gesturing to his brother. Derek was definitely working the room, chatting to whichever lady was close by and even making the married ones blush and laugh. Just a bit shorter than James, his dark hair was like his brother's but a bit longer over the ears, and Amanda could tell that he was used to schmoozing any female that came near to him, with devastating results.

"Lady killer?"

James restrained the urge to roll his eyes. "We try not to use that term in my profession unless it means something entirely different. Just don't wander away with my brother, okay? Once he finds out that you're single and new in town you don't stand a chance."

New in town or not, Amanda still bristled a bit. "Think I can take care of myself, thank you very much! Besides, he's not that good-looking anyway."

"Liar."

She laughed, caught in her little falsehood, and finally agreed with him. "Okay, deal."

Chapter 25

Someone had cranked up the old jukebox in the back room, and one of the Hortman brothers was dancing with his red-haired wife to an Elvis Presley song blaring from the speakers. It didn't take long until a few more people joined in, laughing as they tried to avoid bumping into the other couples. Mrs. Granger watched, seemingly amused, until she pulled herself up into her walker and announced that she wanted to give it a go, too. The crowd parted for her as she headed for the jukebox and started shaking her hips and shuffling to the rock 'n roll music.

James laughed and held out a hand to Amanda. "Want to?" he asked and wordlessly pulled her toward the dancers. It was silly dancing, with a lot of shaking and shuffling and laughing. Amanda tried to do her best to keep up, and it was immediately apparent that her partner was a fabulous dancer. He effortlessly twirled her, then tried to show her how to duck under his arm. She laughed her way through the sudden move and did okay until she smacked into the back of Mrs. Mason, who gave her a disapproving look as she danced away.

They'd been dancing for only a few minutes when Amanda heard a commotion in the back room and someone exclaiming over whatever had happened. People were moving toward the buffet table and Lisa rushed for the café's front door while frantically punching a number onto the screen of her cell phone. James must've heard it too, or maybe he was so tall that he was able to see over the crowd. He grabbed

Amanda's hand and pulled her toward the back room, weaving through people as if he was ready to take charge.

Amanda heard the whispers as she pushed her way through the people to see what had happened. Mayor Sandford, a lady who was always impeccably groomed and elegant in public, was sprawled face down on the floor. Her legs were splayed apart, and she appeared unconscious. James jumped forward and placed his fingers on her neck, feeling for a pulse.

"What happened? Did anyone see her fall?" Seemingly satisfied that she was alive he scanned the crowd. Grace TwoHorses, still clutching a cake server, was nearly in tears.

"She was just talking to me about how Ravenwood Cove has become so full of tourists, and then she seemed to pass out. I couldn't catch her before she hit the floor."

James turned aside. "She's still breathing. Who called 911?"

Just then they could hear the high whine of the ambulance siren. Having the emergency services downtown in a small town sometimes meant it was only moments from the time help was called until it arrived, and Amanda was relieved to see the ambulance double parking in front of the café. James' brother, Derek, helped make a path through the crowd for the paramedics and gurney. As soon as they reached the mayor's side they began to quickly check her over, and calling in to their dispatch center to confirm that they were transporting her to the hospital as quickly as possible.

It took only a few minutes to gently flip the mayor face up and move her to the waiting gurney. As the ambulance pulled away from the curb, patient safely inside and on her way to the nearest hospital, James turned quietly to Ruby and said, "Get me a couple of large ziptop plastic bags, maybe gallon size. Also a big paper grocery bag if you've got one."

Amanda turned, her eyebrows drawn together in confusion. "What do you need bags for?"

James's face looked tired and almost angry. "For her cup of punch. Her plate, too. I think she's been poisoned." Ruby gasped and scuttled into the back room in search of bags.

Mrs. Granger hefted herself out of her chair and gripped her wheeled walker, obviously ready to go. "Well, that's all the fun I can stand to have today. Remind me to do that again sometime, like when I turn a hundred. Meg, get the car."

Amanda handed the old lady her purse. "I'm really sorry this happened at your party, Mrs. Granger."

The elderly woman grinned. "Are you kidding? That was is the most excitement I've had in years! Do me a favor and bring some of that leftover cake to the general store tomorrow, okay? And uh, fill me in on any of the juicy details that I'm gonna miss."

Amanda couldn't even smile as she promised to do just that. James was conferring with George, the police chief, and it was less than five minutes before two more police officers arrived. James gave them some quick, quiet instructions and they began to interview a few of the partygoers.

Ruby hurried back through the crowd, and James took the proffered bags. He pulled a pen out of his pocket and put it through the handle of the empty punch glass, lifting it up and settling it into a plastic bag. He set the pen aside and carefully pressed the zippered top shut, then stashed the mayor's plate in a bag, too. Once they were both put into a large brown paper bag and he'd rolled the top down twice, Amanda's curiosity got the best of her.

"Who do you think did it?" Amanda asked, fully aware that there were people still loitering around, hoping to overhear any details.

"Could've been anyone at the party, and anyone who had motive. That means probably half the town." James straightened up and looked Amanda square in the eye. "Including you."

Amanda's mouth dropped open, stunned. "You can't believe I did this! There were about a hundred people here tonight, and any one of them could've had the opportunity."

James leaned closer, his voice dropped a whisper. "Yes, opportunity, but you had motive, Amanda. You are the only one who was just seen in public, yelling at the mayor about how awful she was. I know maybe other people have yelled at her, too, but I have to include everyone." He paused. "Even the ones I like."

She could feel her heartbeat flutter a bit in her throat as he stood just a little too close to her, holding her gaze just a little too long.

His eyes are the color of a stormy ocean, she thought.

'I...okay." Amanda took a half step back. Standing too close to this guy, a police detective, felt too good and also way too dangerous.

Lisa Wilkins plopped into a nearby chair and let out a sigh of exhaustion. James turned to her. "Lisa, you were greeting people at the door for most of the night, right?" She nodded and James was back in detective mode immediately. "I know some people have already left, but I want you to grab a pen and paper and write down the names of every single person you can remember who was here. Start with the people who are still here, and add as much as you can remember. Amanda might be able to help you. Jot down anything weird you might have seen."

"So, it's still okay for people to leave, right? I didn't even think about having everyone stay."

It only took a few minutes to write down the names of the guests at Mrs. Granger's party, even as they were answering questions from the stragglers who were trying to be part of the action. Amanda could hear James back in the kitchen, talking on his cell phone and giving instructions to a police officer as he snooped around the food prep area.

Lisa was listing everyone she could remember on a yellow pad of paper. "The Ortizes had already left because little Lucy was crying. The Hortman brothers went home early because they said there wasn't enough liquor. Mrs. Granger was sitting in that one chair all night and didn't have the opportunity to do anything except sit in her chair and be the birthday girl. Um, except for when she was dancing."

Amanda's thoughts were going a different direction. "Who had access to the mayor's food?" Lisa looked surprised, but Amanda continued. "I mean, who could've poisoned her? We may not know motives but we can at least try to figure out who had opportunity."

Lisa thought for a moment, her pen tapping on the tabletop as she mulled over her new friend's question. "Well, if there was poison, it couldn't have been in the buffet. Everyone ate from that and the mayor's the only one who wound up face down on the floor."

"Did she go back for seconds? Maybe someone targeted her after the main buffet had been eaten."

Lisa's eyes lit up, remembering. "I did see her go back for a third helping of Grace TwoHorse's stewed tomatoes. I was cleaning the table a bit, trying to wipe up any spilled food, when I saw Mrs. Sandford dishing up more." She shivered in disgust. "Honestly, I have no idea how she could eat something that slimy. Yuck!"

Amanda felt a surge of excitement at Lisa's words. Maybe they were on the right track. "Was anyone else close to her, like close enough to be able to drop some poison in those tomatoes? It wasn't a very popular dish, was it?"

"No, it wasn't. Maybe someone poisoned the tomatoes."

"Anything else?"

Lisa frowned, trying to remember. "She had cake, but I think Emma gave that to her and it was the same time everyone else had cake." There was a pause, then she looked up at Amanda, her face stricken. "There's just one more thing I can remember."

"Yes?" Amanda could hear the dread in her friend's voice.

"I saw Brian Petrie give the mayor a glass of the tropical punch before dinner."

Chapter 26

Some days, you just need to have an impromptu wine party at home with girlfriends.

Amanda was lying on her back on the oriental carpet, her sock-covered feet propped up in the nearest upholstered chair, as she explained her latest batch of theories to Lisa and Meg.

She tried not to wave her hands too much, or she'd knock over her nearly-empty wineglass. "So now I've got a weird Russian neighbor, a store owner who openly loathed the dead guy, and a mayor who hates me. I still think she might be the killer of the guy who was buried in my garden, and then some lowlife poisons the broad at a public gathering." She sat up just enough to take a sip from her glass. "This town is really strange."

Meg cocked an eyebrow at her. "Feel better, propping your feet up like that?"

Amanda reached over to pet Oscar, who was lying by her hip and purring like a happy buzz saw.

"Yes, yes, I do. If I just had chocolate cream pie, I'd be all set."

"Do you have any?" Meg sounded hopeful.

"Nope, but I sure wish I did."

Lisa and Meg laughed, obviously agreeing, and Amanda continued.

"That birthday party tonight was more than I can take. You know how many times someone got poisoned and keeled over at a party when I was at in LA? Zero. Nada. Zilch."

Lisa sighed wistfully. "What are LA parties like?"

"Boring. Full of people who talk like they're reciting their resumes and telling you all the ways you should fear and revere them." Amanda turned her head toward her friend, surprised. "You don't mean you'd want to move to LA, do you?"

Lisa shrugged ruefully. "No, but I just was wondering if there were a lot of movie stars at LA parties. You know, kinda elegant and important."

"No movie stars I saw. Just guys on the make and tons of lonely people."

There was a pause while they all thought about that, then Meg piped up, "Yeah, but at least they don't have stewed tomatoes on the buffet table."

Amanda grinned. "Well, you may have a point."

Lisa wasn't going to be swayed. "Amanda, what are you going to do now? We've got one person murdered, one person poisoned...maybe...and the mayor blocking you opening your business. I can't see how you can-"

Her friend interrupted, sitting up and crossing her legs. "Look, I can only keep moving forward the best I can. The thought of having to crawl back to LA with my tail between my legs just kills me. I don't have much of a choice but to stay here and try to find out who's behind all this."

"Is that why you're not just selling the Inn, instead of going through all this trouble? Look, I'm glad you're staying, but – "

Amanda put a hand up to stop Lisa's words. "I've thought about it, but I'm not selling because this is my home now, and I'm tired of moving every few years. Also, the Inn is the last piece of my family history that I own and if I sell it to someone else they'll just bulldoze it and sell the land." She played with the stem of her wineglass, thinking. "I'm not going to just throw it away because someone is trying to push me. I really hate being pushed."

The next words nearly stuck in her throat. "I don't have any other real family, so the Inn's all I have left."

Meg shook her head, disagreeing. "Sometimes family isn't the people you grew up with. Sometimes it's the people you meet who become part of you."

Amanda sighed. "I wish that were true."

Oscar chose that moment to try to rub against Lisa's wineglass, knocking it over onto the white sweatshirt she'd taken off earlier and tossed onto the floor. There was a general outcry and rush of hands to try to keep the dark wine from spilling onto the carpet as they rolled the stained sweatshirt into a ball, trapping the liquid inside.

Disaster averted, Amanda sprawled into a nearby chair, still considering Lisa's question. "Whatever we talk about here has to stay confidential, okay? I need to talk about this and not worry it's gonna show up on the front page the next day." She shook a warning finger at Lisa. "Promise?"

"I promise. Anything we talk about here stays in this room."

Maybe it was the wine or maybe it was how well her new friends listened, but Amanda spilled out the entire story of how Crescent Crown Company was trying to build a huge retirement resort that would basically take over the entire town. She told them about the fact that Petrie's hardware store tape had been used to wrap the body, the results of the autopsy, and the letter she'd found. By the time she got to the part about the mayor owning the land that was being considered for the resort, Lisa and Meg both had their mouths hanging open in shock.

"You have *got* to be kidding me. So that's what you meant about someone bulldozing the Inn," Lisa said, and Meg nodded her head in silent agreement.

"I would've brought the information to you, Lisa, but I was worried that this sort of news story might've killed off the last bit of tourist trade we had, and all the local shop owners would've gone out of business."

"Well, if the mayor didn't kill Emmett, then who did?"

Lisa sighed. "Brian seems like such a nice guy. I just can't believe he'd have anything to do with Emmett's death."

Amanda poured herself a bit more wine. "I think people can do all sorts of horrible things and still appear to be Nice Guys. Brian told me himself that Emmett had messed with his sister. Protecting family can bring out violence in lots of people and maybe Brian's one of them."

"Yeah, but why would he have a beef with the mayor?" Lisa asked, obviously mulling it over.

"Maybe he was getting tired of being told what to do with his store. You know the town council turned down his proposal to expand into a greenhouse, and he's probably been the most vocal of any of the townspeople about how bad the mayor's rulings have been for business. Even if there's been an improvement since all that publicity with the shells and stuff started, maybe he wants more money."

Meg nodded, obviously agreeing. "She's probably done all sorts of things we don't know about anyway. If she's so sneaky that she'd file a rezoning...whatever it's called... to get the Ravenwood turned into just a house, who knows what else she's got up her sleeve?"

Meg picked up her wineglass and took a sip. "You know, the mayor could still be the killer. Maybe someone is trying to shut her up." She turned to her friend Lisa, who was happily petting the cat. "And here's a weird thought, but you could be a suspect, too, Lisa. You were the one who wrote that article about what was going on in the town and how the city council wasn't serving the voters the way they should." At the instant outcry of protest, Meg threw up her hands as if to shush them, but continued. "You put your anger out there for the whole town to read about, and no one else had done that."

Lisa scoffed, obviously offended. "I was only writing what most people already were thinking. Anyone who read that article and had a beef with the mayor would've had motive, so that means there would be

174

dozens of suspects. Count me out. My way of getting even is what I write, not who I'd poison."

Oscar's purring was the only sound in the room as they all digested this statement.

"And what about the letter?" Lisa asked. "If the mayor didn't kill Emmett, then who wrote that threatening letter?"

"Well, whoever it was, we know it *wasn't* my uncle 'cause the handwriting wasn't the same. I don't have any problem with the idea of the cops figuring out who's behind that letter."

"Yeah, you wouldn't have any problem with that because you get to talk to some cute sheriff detective guy, right?" Meg winked at Amanda, who completely ignored her.

"You know that letter bothers me. It said that they wanted my uncle to get out of town. I guess the question is why? How would that benefit the person who wrote it if my family *did* leave Ravenwood Cove?"

Meg shrugged. "Maybe blackmail, anger, get them out of the way. Maybe they wanted the land, too."

Amanda flopped back on the floor, frustrated. "Sometimes I think I'll never figure this out, with my aunt and uncle dead. There must be some way to put the pieces together."

Always practical, Lisa summed up the unspoken thoughts of them all. "Well, whether the mayor is the killer or not, we now know that someone in town is a potential murderer." She turned toward her friend, still lying on the floor. "And that means they could be coming after you, too. I don't like the idea of you being in the Inn all by yourself at night. If you want, I can stay over some nights and keep you company."

"Me, too!" Meg's face was unusually serious.

Amanda shook her head. "Guys, I really appreciate the offer but I'm okay. Besides," she held up Oscar, who looked terribly annoyed. "-I've got Oscar to protect me."

No one laughed at her little joke, and Lisa's voice was nearly stern when she caught Amanda's eye.

"Someone's killed before, and someone's tried to kill again. They were at that party and it means they're still in this town."

"I guess I'll just have to watch my back."

"I'm more worried about who's going to be watching yours." Lisa's voice was deadly serious. "And if anyone wants to stick a knife in it."

Chapter 27

After she waved goodbye to her girlfriends and locked up the Inn, Amanda put on her pajamas and headed to bed. It took longer than it should have to fall asleep, as she thought back over the night's conversation. She tried counting backwards and doing relaxation exercises but just as she'd drift off the sound of the wind or her own tangled thoughts would wake her. It was probably her imagination, but the Inn seemed to be creaking more than normal in the night wind, flexing as if it was complaining about its age. Snug inside, Amanda could still hear every small noise around her as she tossed and turned, finally waking again just before dawn to the sound of a car door shutting outside. The quiet slam jerked her awake and she shuffled to the window, peering around the heavy drapes to the front yard.

Jennifer Peetman's car was parked next door at Mrs. Petrovski's house, the brake lights still on as Jennifer walked around to the driver's side. Amanda could just make out the Russian lady's form in the passenger seat, clutching a bag. Instead of opening her own door Jennifer walked to the back and popped the trunk open. Only then did Amanda see what she was carrying in her hand. It was a full-sized shovel, the heavy old-fashioned type, and she quickly stashed it and closed the trunk door.

Why on earth would her neighbor be out with Jennifer at this hour in the morning, and with a shovel? Amanda was suddenly, completely awake as her mind whirled, trying to sort out possibilities. She couldn't help but flash back to all the shovels the police had been using as they had dug up the remains in her garden, or the sound of digging as they had sifted through yards of dirt looking for additional clues.

She was short on clues and needed any information she could get. She grabbed her car keys and pounded down the stairs, startling Oscar, who had been sleeping on the parlor sofa. By the time she was outside and had jammed the key in the ignition, she remembered that she was only wearing her thin pajamas and slippers. Cranking up the car's heater to try to dispel the chill, she turned out of her circular driveway and down the hill, following Jennifer's car. She could just see the tail lights ahead of her, moving at a good clip through the town. Amanda's heart was thumping as she followed as far back as she could, trying to avoid being seen by keeping as much distance between them as possible while still not losing them.

Jennifer's little car didn't seem to be going in any one direction. Even with staying behind her as far as she was, Amanda could tell that the car ahead of her was zigzagging through the streets of Ravenwood Cove. At first Amanda thought that the car in front of her had seen her headlights, so she slowed down and hung back, but after the third time that Jennifer's car veered off in an unexpected direction, Amanda suddenly realized that it couldn't be because the driver saw her every time. It was as though Jennifer was trying to evade whoever might be following her.

Like she was hiding a secret and didn't want to be followed.

Like she had done this sort of driving before.

Amanda could feel her heartbeat hammering in her chest as she realized that whatever her neighbor was involved with, it certainly wasn't something legal. Hesitantly, she turned off her car lights, trying not to be seen, but the windy night was still dark enough that once she was away from the antique streetlights of Ravenwood Cove's tiny downtown area, she didn't have enough light to see the road ahead of her. Jennifer's tail lights blinked once as they pulled around a corner and then disappeared as the car went down a hill, toward the beach.

Amanda sat the darkness, still-icy air blowing across her thin clothing, and her eyes boring into the night as if she could summon the little car back. After a moment she resigned herself to the fact she'd lost, turned her car lights back on, and made a U-turn toward the Inn.

She doubted she'd get any more sleep that night.

Chapter 28

It felt kind of weird to walk into the hospital clutching a bouquet of carnations, but Amanda was determined. Maybe the mayor was her enemy, and maybe she was the reason Amanda didn't have any income, but Amanda was never going to get to the bottom of what was going on until she did some more investigation.

Enemy or not, Mayor Sandford may have been poisoned by the same person who killed Emmet, and that meant that she might have clues that Amanda needed.

After stopping at the nurse's station for directions, she turned left toward the main block of rooms. The halls were empty and smelled faintly of antiseptic. At the final turn Amanda was surprised to find a very familiar figure standing outside the mayor's hospital room.

"James, what are you doing here?"

His eyebrows went up when he spotted the flowers she was carrying. "I could ask you the same thing. Not going to strangle her in her sleep are you?"

She gasped. "That's a terrible thing to say, especially after what you said about me being a suspect!" She thrust the flowers at him. "Here! You give these to her. I've got better things to do."

His words stung, but it was easier to be mad and offended than go along with his little jest. He put his hands out to catch her arm as she whipped around, ready to head out the nearest exit. His voice was apologetic when he said, "Sorry, Amanda. I was just kidding."

She looked at him sideways, still mad. To his credit, he looked suitably contrite so she shook off his hand and stepped back. "Okay." She took a deep breath. "It still wasn't funny, though."

"I can take in those flowers for you if you want. Right now she's sleeping." At her answering nod, he pushed open the hospital room door and quietly set the bright floral arrangement on the windowsill.

Amanda couldn't tear her eyes away from the small, rumpled form sleeping in the bed. Mrs. Sandford looked kind of gray and drawn, as if her age and her unhappy life had suddenly caught up to her. She seemed much less ferocious than usual, and was snoring lightly in between slow breaths.

Flowers deposited, James ushered Amanda outside and silently clicked the door shut. He was watching Amanda's face, realizing that seeing the mayor in this state must've been a very different sort of encounter than Amanda had ever had with the old woman.

"She looks so frail." Amanda was almost whispering, as if her voice would wake her, even though the door was closed.

He nodded, understanding.

Amanda cleared her throat. "Um, any clue on what happened? Or who might've done it?"

"Well, we know that they found a partially-digested piece of candy in her stomach when she was admitted to the hospital. Tests on it showed a strong poison that would only take minutes to affect a victim."

"Candy?" Amanda looked puzzled. "So it wasn't the punch?" He shook his head and she continued. "Did you learn anything else about who may have done it? Who would want to poison her?"

James gestured to a group of chairs down the hall and Amanda followed him, plopping down with a sigh. "Look, the mayor isn't exactly the most popular person in town. Could've been a lot of people."

"Even me?"

James turned toward her, a small smile on his lips, seemingly switching from detective mode to friend. "Doubtful. I was with you in the timeframe when the poison would've had to be administered, so I think I can officially rule you out this time."

The sigh of relief seemed to come from her toes. "Whew! Glad you finally figured that out, Detective."

He grinned. "Call it a hunch. You would've just set your attack cat on her. Oscar's big enough he could've taken her out easy."

The laugh felt good, cleansing, even if they had had to stifle themselves a bit so it wasn't too loud for the nearby patients.

"Ravenwood Inn's Attack Cat. Think I'll put that on his collar." Amanda wiped her eyes. "Okay, so if my cat's been cleared, who are your suspects?"

He was instantly all business again. "According to the lab crew, that poison would've taken only minutes so she must've gotten it at the party. I'm going to do some more questioning to see if anyone remembers seeing her eat a piece of candy, but right now everyone at that party is on the suspect list."

"Except me."

His smile was warm. "Except you," he confirmed. The smile became a grin. "Maybe."

She smacked him playfully on the arm. "You know better. So, how is this tied to Emmett's murder?"

"We're not sure that it is. This town hasn't had this much excitement in a long time, but the timing could just be coincidence." At her look of disbelief he patted her on the arm, trying to calm her down. "I know, I know. It does seem really suspicious but I don't have anything conclusive yet. Until we know more I can't rule it out though, either."

James sprawled in the chair, crossing his long legs in front of him. Amanda couldn't help but admire his well-worn cowboy boots.

"Waiting for your horse to come strolling by, Tex?"

"Hey, you try growing up on a horse ranch. Means you get boots before you get sneakers. Also, the pointy toes are great for kicking older brothers, as long as you can outrun 'em after you do it." He wiggled his boot-covered foot, showing it off.

"I wouldn't know. I never had brothers or sisters, so I didn't have anyone to kick."

James laughed softly. "Lady, you are missing out. Bugging my brothers is part of some of my favorite memories. I never would've kicked my sister, but brothers are a whole different ballgame."

A lone nurse walked by on whisper-silent shoes. Once she reached the end of the hall and disappeared down the next corridor James sat up in his chair.

"Amanda, you need to think about this, though. If there is a connection, it means the killer is still around town and for some reason wanted the mayor dead, too. You need to be careful, okay?"

She could see the genuine concern in his eyes, and smiled. "Don't you worry, detective. I can take care of myself."

His look was serious. "I hope so, lady."

Chapter 29

It was warm in James' arms, and when she pressed her ear to his chest, she could hear a strong heartbeat through his flannel shirt. Amanda snuggled deeper, loving the sensation of being so close to him and him holding her. She tilted her head upward, seeing the gleam in his sea-colored eyes as he pulled her toward him, knowing instinctively he was going to press his lips against hers. She wrapped both her arms around his neck, drawing him downward as his mouth was inches from hers. He hesitated for just a second, opening his mouth to speak, and finally said –

COCK A DOODLE DOO!

Amanda jerked upward and slid out of bed onto the hard wooden floor, her arms still wrapped around the large pillow she'd been sleeping with.

A dream. That damn rooster! He had such bad timing...

There was no sunlight peeking through the heavy curtains, so it couldn't be daytime yet, and Amanda squinted at her clock. Two fifteen in the middle of the night! It had sounded like Dumb Cluck had stationed his loud, time-impaired self directly under her windowsill again, and he was still crowing his lungs out, only stopping to breathe for a few seconds between blaring like a siren. He'd never woken her up so early before and this time she had absolutely lost patience with him.

"That's *it*!" she vowed, picking up a boot so she could hurl it at the irritating chicken. "You're going in the stew pot, DC!" She jerked the window open and threw the heavy boot as hard as she could, but the neighborhood's stray rooster veered away like crazy and the shoe missed him by several feet.

Outside the night air was cold and damp, and the lights she'd left on in front of the Inn didn't reach around to the back. She was muttering to herself and just about to pull her head back inside when she smelled something.

Something that shouldn't be there.

It was smoke. Not the type of smoke smell she had gotten used to, when her neighbors were burning their leaves or brush piles, but the familiar smell of a campfire.

Burning wood.

Craning her head around, she could just see a brief flash of flickering light, coming from near the kitchen. With a horrified lurch she pulled her head inside and dove across the bed to grab her cell phone. By the time she'd reached the emergency dispatcher she was already frantically running down the stairs, trying not to slip in her haste, as she barked out the necessary info on the phone.

The Ravenwood Inn! On fire! Come as fast as you can!

Amanda was still desperately babbling into the phone when she grabbed the red fire extinguisher off the kitchen wall. The hungry flames were higher now, their menacing light streaming through the glass pane on the back door. Amanda tried to assess how big the fire was, took a deep breath, and smashed the heavy metal canister against the frosted glass with all her might. It exploded outward with a loud crash and brittle shards blew out onto the porch. A wave of heat from the fire slammed into her through the gaping window frame, and she could see the flames spreading across the porch floor and starting to lick up the railing toward the overhanging roof.

Gasping for air, she frantically pulled the pin on the fire extinguisher. Using the door as a sort of shield against the intense heat she aimed the nozzle through the broken-out window and squeezed the metal trigger, rewarded by a furious rush of white fire retardant. The fire was so hot she had to turn sideways to gulp a breath of air before training the extinguisher on the bottom of the blaze again, and then again. Just as the fire extinguisher started to sputter and cough she heard the amazing, blessed sound of screaming sirens speeding toward the Inn.

The fire was smaller, but still not out. She could hear the first responders hollering to each other and she yelled back. "In the back! On the kitchen porch! Hurry!" She threw the empty extinguisher to the side and ran to fill a soup kettle with water blasting loudly from the kitchen faucet. By the time she ran back to the broken door, sloshing water from the deep pot as she went, two of the firemen had dragged a thick hose toward the back and were bellowing instructions toward the firetruck. A moment of waiting, but an eternity before the water sputtered, then sprayed out of the huge nozzle. It took less than two minutes for the crew to douse the flames completely, then they used their axes to pull up the porch floorboards to make sure that no spark was left, waiting for a chance to flare up again.

Amanda stood just inside the back door, her breath coming in adrenaline-fueled gasps, water dripping down the front of her nightie from the forgotten kettle of water. She'd always been afraid of fire, and to see the evil flames trying to devour her beloved Inn was almost more than she could stand, but she'd stood against it, and she'd fought it. She still wasn't sure how she'd known to pull the pin on the fire extinguisher, but even though she'd been terrified, she had done her best and called for help to do the rest.

Her mother had always told her that too much pride was a bad thing, but for the first time in years that was exactly what Amanda felt. Pride. Pride in fighting the fire, and pride that she'd kept her head enough to call the dispatcher.

A dark-haired figure ran by the firemen and leapt over the hole that had been hacked in the porch floor, skidding to a stop just outside the still-closed door. Amanda grabbed a kitchen towel from the counter and used it to protect her hand on the hot doorknob as she pushed the door open.

James took one look at Amanda's soot-smudged face and instantly scooped her up into a warm hug, just as suddenly putting her down, as if he remembered that he really shouldn't be doing that.

"Are you okay?"

She nodded mutely, her heartbeat still pounding in her ears.

"Um, yes. I have insurance – "

"– No, I mean *okay*," he interrupted. "Are you hurt?"

A small shake of her head and, seemingly satisfied, James surveyed the damage. Two firefighters were still checking for hot spots, but from their chatting and calmness it was apparent that the fire was completely out.

James walked back onto the porch, checking over the entire burnt area. After about a minute deep in thought he gave his opinion. "Looking at the burn mark, it seems like someone doused your back porch in something flammable and lit a match." His eyes caught hers. "I think this is a case of arson, not an accident."

Amanda wasn't really surprised, because somewhere in the back of her mind she'd thought it probably was arson, too. Always cautious with fire, she'd double-checked the electrical system when she moved in and made a nightly before-bed inspection to be sure that the stove and any unneeded lights were turned off. She'd had a fear of fire ever since her mother's fireplace mantle had caught on fire one day when she was seven. Maybe she was the one who had put something so explosive in the trash, she still didn't know, but all she remembered what standing stock-still in horror while her mother ran with a bowl of sloshing water from the kitchen, and doused the flames.

"The rooster," she gasped, "Dumb Cluck woke me up. If he hadn't been crowing his head off in the middle of the night right under my window, I would've slept through it."

"The rooster woke you up?" James looked dumbfounded.

Amanda nodded. "From now on that chicken can crow whenever he wants, and I'll feed him corn *myself*."

The tall detective laughed and glanced back at the damaged porch. "Well, the good news is that we caught it in time, and that there's more brick than wood back here. The fire's out and you're safe. I'll tape off the back porch as a crime scene. This was no accident." His face was grim as he strode back to his car. A minute's rummaging in the trunk and he returned, yellow tape in hand.

"You look exhausted." Amanda couldn't help but notice the sag to his body and the dark circles under his eyes.

"I've had a helluva day. Was dealing with a fatal rollover accident on highway 101, right after an all-day investigation of a child abuse case over at Likely. I've been going nonstop since midnight last night." He stifled a yawn. "I was just heading home when I heard the call over my radio."

"Gotten any sleep at all?"

"No, but if you sing me a lullaby I'll probably just curl up on your counter and start snoring there."

"Sounds charming." Amanda looked closer and realized that James didn't just look exhausted; he looked sick. She walked over and set her palm gently on his cheek. "Detective Landon, you are burning up. You're probably running a fever of over a hundred."

"I'm okay. Just too much time out in the weather."

Her eyebrows raised in disapproval. "You should be home in bed." When he didn't look surprised she instantly guessed why. "You know you're sick, don't you?"

He shrugged. "No one else to fill in today, so what was I supposed to do?" He walked into the kitchen and pulled out a clean dishtowel, ran it under the water and walked over to Amanda.

"Here. Soot on your face." He dabbed at a spot on her forehead, then handed her the damp towel, watching as she scrubbed dutifully under his watchful gaze.

She could tell he was mulling over something. "I think this was to scare you, or maybe to do enough damage that you'd leave." He gestured toward the back porch, small tendrils of smoke still spiraling upward from the water-logged wood. "If they'd wanted to hurt or kill you there are lots of more efficient ways than to burn the porch off the Inn. The sunroom is mostly wood, with wood siding above it, and would've made it more difficult to view from the front. It would've gone up like a torch if they'd started a fire there. This area has a lot of brick around it."

James cleared his throat, knowing she wasn't going to like what he was going to say.

"Look, I'm going to sleep in my car in the driveway, so I know you're protected. I don't think they'll be back to do any more damage but I'd rather be safe than sorry."

Amanda brushed the hanging hair back from her face. "I really appreciate it, James, but you're in no condition to do that." She plopped down onto a stool by the kitchen island and sighed. "You said yourself that you thought the fire wasn't meant to hurt me; just scare me. After everything that's gone on tonight I won't get to sleep for hours and by the time I do it'll probably be dawn. There's really no need for you to stay."

"I'll be fine."

"Detective, you're sick."

As James started to protest he was interrupted by the young cop coming in the back door. "I could stay," he said eagerly.

James shook his head. "Rollins, you've already been assigned a patrol shift. How are you going to cover that and stay here?"

"My shift ends in half an hour and I could just stay out front until daylight. That way you can to go home and get better, and I get a few hours of overtime, if the sheriff's office will pay outta their budget. That work for you, detective?"

Amada looked back toward James, and at last he nodded. "That will be fine, Rollins, but I want your word that you won't leave the premises. Deal?"

At the rookie's eager nod James stuck out his hand and shook with the younger cop. "Thanks, buddy. I feel terrible," he finally admitted. "I'm going home."

"Good. Thanks for coming by, James. I really do appreciate it." Amanda smiled at the tall detective as she ushered him out the front door. Just as she was about to close it behind him he stopped and leaned back inside.

"I'll have the ringer on my phone turned up so I can hear it if you call." He yawned again, covering his open mouth with his hand. "I just need a couple of hours of sleep, and I'll be back in the morning. We can talk things over then, okay?"

Amanda watched him out of the window, not surprised to see that he did a final walk around the grounds to check for anything suspicious before he drove away.

With the police and firefighters gone, Amanda's previous prediction about not being able to sleep proved to be true. She tried wrapping herself in a quilt on the parlor sofa but her mind was still racing with the memories of what had happened that night. Every once in awhile she'd get up to peek out the front window, where the patrol car sat like a protective pit bull. After about an hour of restless fidgeting Amanda finally admitted defeat.

With a sigh she opened the fridge and started pulling out ingredients. If she couldn't sleep she might as well bake something. The firefighters and police had done an amazing job with the fire, and the least she could do was take them a huge batch of fresh chocolate chip cookies to thank them.

Oven on, mixing bowl and measuring cups and spoons pulled out, ingredients all over the kitchen island, and she was in business. She'd used the same cookie recipe since she was a child and her mother was teaching her how to cook; gently correcting her from dropping bits of eggshell in the dough and letting her lick the spoon and bowl afterward. The memory was a nice break in what had been an awful night, and Amanda lost herself in the rhythm of measuring and mixing the ingredients. She remembered all the times she'd rolled out dough to make Christmas or Halloween sugar cookies, each cookie carefully decorated so she could share them with family and friends.

When it was time to put in the dry ingredients she dug a cup into the bag of powdery-soft flour and dumped it into a new bowl. It landed with a nearly-silent *poof,* dusty bits gently settled onto the bowl's sides, and something suddenly clicked in Amanda's brain.

Flour.

Flour on Emmett. On the murdered body.

Halloween cookies.

Her mouth dropped open, the measuring cup forgotten in her hand. Means, motive, and opportunity. That's what made a murder.

It had been right in front of Amanda's face all along but only now were the pieces of the puzzle starting to fit together.

I have to tell James, she thought, reaching for her phone, but suddenly remembered how exhausted and feverish the detective had been. She knew Rollins was still sitting out front so she felt safe, and she didn't want to wake James by calling him. Her news could wait. Amanda's fingers hovered over the screen for a split second, and then she started tapping quickly, sending James a short text.

Have important information! Call me or stop by when you're up.

By the time Amanda had mixed together everything for the cookie dough, she was feeling waves of exhaustion washing over her. Even with everything that had happened in the middle of the night, Amanda's adrenaline could only go so far. Deciding that she'd have time to bake the next day, Amanda put a plate on top of the bowl of chocolate chip cookie dough and put in the fridge, sneaking a taste just before she closed the door.

Plenty of time to bake cookies after I get some sleep, she thought. Stifling a yawn, she shuffled back to the parlor couch. As soon as she lay down she could feel the fatigue pulling her deeper into the plush cushions, and she wrapped the quilt back around herself and rolled over. She was almost asleep when she felt a cautious paw placed on her calf as her new cat slowly stepped across the quilt and snuggled into the curves of her body, as if she wouldn't notice if he was just quiet enough.

Amanda sighed happily and reached down to pet Oscar's head. Amazing how some things in life could be made better by just chocolate chip cookie dough and a purring cat tucked behind her knees. With the promise of a new morning and new revelations to tell James, she finally sank into dreamless sleep.

Chapter 30

The hand-written note was shoved through the old mail slot in the Inn's front door, and was short and to the point.

I peeked in but didn't want to wake you. Would love to buy you breakfast at the Cannery today on Oceanside road so we can talk things over. My treat, meet me at 9. They've got the best oysters in town.

Oysters for breakfast, she thought, and shuddered. *He must be feeling better. Doubt those'll be my cup of tea.* Just reading the words in the note made her smile. After she'd started putting clues together last night she had a list of things to tell James, and she was sure it would be a breakfast that he wouldn't forget.

Hope he got enough sleep, she thought. She texted a confirmation to James that she would meet him for breakfast at 9 o'clock and fed Oscar, who was patrolling the kitchen and loudly reminding her about his missing breakfast. Carefully locking the front door, she jogged out to her car, threw in her purse and started on her way. A morning drizzle had set in and she had to turn on her windshield wipers as she drove through town, the overcast sky settling over the coastal village like a thick blanket.

She had a vague idea where the Cannery restaurant was, but when she saw Mrs. Mason setting out the wooden sandwich board sign for the Bake Me Happy bakery, she pulled over to the sidewalk and rolled down her window.

"Good morning, Mrs. Mason!" she called cheerfully, hoping the older lady wasn't hard of hearing.

"Oh, good morning, Amanda. Not exactly California weather, is it?" Mrs. Mason gestured to the damp sky with disgust.

Amanda couldn't help but smile. "Actually, I think I'm getting used to the Pacific Northwest rain. I'm sorry to bother you, but I was wondering if you could point me toward the Cannery restaurant? I'm supposed to meet someone there and I'm not sure where it is, exactly."

Mrs. Mason wiped her hands, covered with bits of dough and flour, on her new pink and white striped apron, just as her phone rang. She pulled it out of her pocket and hastily told Amanda, "Down the street, turn right on Elm and follow it to the beach. About a half mile or so down and it's on the left, right on the old pier. Restaurant's in the front of the building, and the cannery's in the back."

The road to the beach bent north, toward Likely, and wound down to sea-level through a scrubby forest. Amanda took her time, watching for potholes as she drove over the rough asphalt. It took her only a few minutes to drive the rest of the way to the restaurant, and she could see right away that the place included a small cannery at the back of the building, and an old covered pier attached at the side, probably to facilitate getting the seafood into the cannery and then available for loading onto trucks going to market.

She was starting to turn left into the gravel parking lot when her world exploded.

There was a rush of movement out of the corner of her eye and she turned just in time to see a large gray SUV screech out of a forested side street and accelerate full speed into the side of her car. The crash was monumental, as the sounds of tearing metal and exploding glass hit Amanda as hard the air bag smashing into her upper body and face.

Her head flopped back, there was a moment of high-pitched buzzing in her ears, and then the sudden silence was deafening. Just as her thoughts were beginning to clear the driver car door was yanked open and someone was frantically cutting through her seatbelt.

Charles.

She gasped as the wiry lawyer leapt forward, grabbed her arm and throat and yanked her roughly out of the wrecked car. She tried to shift her weight as he changed his relentless grip on her torso and wrapped his other arm tightly around her neck. She was stunned at how strong his desperation and rage had made him, and she instantly tried to dig her fingers into the groove around her neck, frantic to pull the arm blocking her windpipe away.

Air. She needed to breathe!

He was dragging her, the heels of her boots banging and scraping as she kicked and fought, straining for any bit of oxygen she could get into her compressed windpipe. She was frantic, twisting and thrashing as she tried to get leverage or any way to kick or punch him, as he slowly pulled her farther and farther into the cold darkness of the long, covered pier. She caught glimpses of bushel boxes and crab traps that had been pushed along the walls, stored for the cannery that was at the back of the restaurant.

She'd never thought much about death but she knew, absolutely knew, that he was going to kill her without any mercy, without a thought for her pain or terror. If she could only stop him somehow, try to get him to ease up enough to let her twist free...

"Flour mill."

It was all she could gasp out, but it stopped Charles in his tracks for moment.

"Well, you figured out something, didn't you, girlie?"

As he stood still, she stopped thrashing, desperately hoping that her words could somehow stop him, could bring him back to reason. She tried to keep her voice even and calm.

"You weren't at a conference on that Halloween. *You* were the one who told the police about my uncle yelling at Emmett, so you had to be in town."

She gulped for air, dark spots swimming in front of her eyes, her nails digging into the hard flesh of the huge arm clenched across her neck.

"Emmett...you killed him. Somehow, at your family's mill..."

"What if I did, huh?" he hissed in her ear, his hot breath smelling of peppermint. "You really think the world would miss a bastard like that, who think he owns the world, do ya? Suffocation in a flour bin was too good for him."

So that was how it had happened.

He began to drag her again, clenching her to him with nearly superhuman strength. Amanda's oxygen-starved brain was weaving her thoughts together almost randomly as she struggled against the psychopath relentlessly pulling her toward the darkness, and towards her death. She struggled to stay alert, desperately searching for something that would make her murderer stop.

"You hated Emmett...why?" she ground out. "What was he doing to you?"

The arm of iron tightened around her chest. "Let's just say I was tired of him bleeding me dry."

He shifted the weight of her body against his, then continued dragging her down the warped planks of the pier. Amanda could hear the rolling waves crashing beneath the rows of pillars sunk into the sand so far below her. The darkness of the pier wrapped around them as he reached the end, stopping in front of abandoned boxes and broken crab pots.

"I had my reasons for doing what I did." His voice sounded belligerent and defensive. "God only knows how many people Emmett was blackmailing."

There it was. Blackmail was the reason Charles had killed Emmett.

"What did you do, Charles?" Her words must've struck a chord, because Charles suddenly clutched her so tightly that it felt as if her ribs cracked under the pressure. Amanda bit her lip to keep from yelping in pain.

"Not my fault that the new DA was over enthusiastic about the Jefferson case, or that my client needed a break to get acquitted." He paused, breathing heavily. "Not my fault that I figured out how to get some of the evidence out of the locker or that Emmett found it in my office."

"So you buried him at the Inn, hoping it might implicate my family."

His grin was evil and full of teeth. "Extra insurance in case I needed it. I figured he'd be found some day and then there was no way your uncle could get around that. I wanted th^ inn and nothing was going to stop me."

Oh God. She suddenly realized that under the seemingly-perfect exterior and public image of a kind small-town lawyer was a soul that was dark with greed and twisted hatred.

"I made a mistake putting him in the ground. The sea should've eaten him." His breath was coming fast and hard. She could feel his blood racing through the arm of iron that he had clamped across her neck. "I won't make the same mistake twice."

"Candy. You gave the mayor one of your mints at the party –" Maybe if she kept him talking she could think of something.

"– And she still didn't die!" Charles interrupted. "How can I get control of her estate if I can't get that woman out of the way?"

His face was close to hers, the stubble on his unshaved cheek grinding into the soft skin by her ear. So close.

Close enough. She'd only get one chance.

She gathered every bit of breath she had, every ounce of strength and courage and twisted her neck enough that she could sink her teeth mercilessly into his florid face, biting down savagely.

His scream was wild and high, full of rage and pain as he adjusted his grip on her, but she slammed the heel of her riding boot backward desperately into his knee. With a yelp of agony, he lurched sideways and she squirmed away from him, under his arms and ducking forward, running for her very life.

She could hear him moving around, trying to leap to his feet to stop her from escaping. To kill her.

Her legs pumped wildly as she imagined his long fingers grabbing the air behind her, trying to catch her flying hair, closing in by inches. She had gotten only a few yards away when she heard a resounding crack and a loud thump on the creaky wooden floorboards.

A thump like a falling body. She took a couple more staggering steps before she realized that only silence was behind her, that no one was charging after her.

She turned her head just enough to see what had happened, and then skidded to a stop, her breath catching in her throat. Behind her, Charles was folded over on the pier, unconscious, a thin line of blood coming from his head.

And standing over him with a shovel in her hand was her Russian neighbor. She was breathing heavily, her legs splayed apart as if bracing herself from falling or in case of further battle, and her headscarf askew.

Amanda had never seen Mrs. Petrovski anywhere except in the Inn's orchard or welcoming Jennifer into her home next door. She was absolutely the last person Amanda would've guessed would be inside the covered pier first thing in the morning. Scanning around her, Amanda could now see that there were mussels, probably freshly-gathered, scattered widely over the floor, and a place back behind a stack of boxes that was probably where her odd, old neighbor had been hiding.

Or waiting or reading, or whatever she was actually doing.

"Thank you thank you thank you!" The words were a gasping tumble from her mouth as she tried to catch her breath and thank the squat lady all at once.

In the distance, she could just hear the faint whine of a police siren, the noise ebbing and rising with the ocean wind. Mrs. Petrovski's eyes went wide at the sound and she gripped her shovel tightly as she swiveled her head around toward the opening the floor. A rusted steel ladder dropped downward through the hole, probably toward a lower level of the cannery, hidden by the bulk of the pier.

"I...I'll come talk to you later! I promise!" Amanda's savior said, and then ran at the ladder to shimmy down as fast as possible.

Only...it hadn't been the voice of a woman at all. The bundled up neighbor who'd helped save Amanda's life had the gruff, deep voice of a man. A husky voice of someone who may have smoked for years, and who definitely did not have a Russian accent.

Even his running hadn't looked like the gait of a woman. He had lumbered quickly toward the ladder with an absolutely masculine step. Mrs. Petrovski was absolutely, positively some guy who was hiding in broad daylight and living right next door to her Inn.

Someone who was desperately afraid of the police.

By the time James' car skidded to a stop in the restaurant's parking lot, Amanda had grabbed the heavy shovel and was standing over the unmoving lawyer, the adrenaline of the last ten minutes still coursing through her body. She kept glancing from Charles to the pier's opening, praying that the big detective would get to her before the killer would wake.

James was coming toward her at a sprinter's run, gun drawn. The moment he was able to grab her arm and pull her away from Charles, her defenses and all her panic suddenly collapsed, and she let James push her behind him, his gun still pointing toward the figure lying on the ground.

Amanda tried not to sob as James leaned over and pressed his fingers onto Charles' jugular, checking for a pulse.

"I've called for backup but we'll need an ambulance. Call 911!" he bellowed, and Amanda instantly remembered that her purse with her phone was probably still in her wrecked car.

She turned to run for her phone but at that very moment, Charles sprang upward like a man possessed and made a desperate leap toward the open hole in the pier's floor, trying to dive toward the metal ladder. James lurched forward after him, his fingers inches from Charles' coat, but just as he almost grabbed him there was a terrible crack of lumber and Charles screamed shrilly as the rotten flooring split in two under his driving footsteps. He slammed downward into the new opening, his fingers desperately scrabbling at the pitted boards, but it was futile and he crashed down, out of sight. Amanda stifled the small scream that she didn't know came up in her throat, her hand on her mouth, as she heard the terrible, heavy thud of a body hitting the rocks and timbers far below.

James put a hand back to hold Amanda in place, maybe to protect her from falling or maybe to keep her from seeing the grisly scene beneath them. He leaned forward toward the broken edges of the hole carefully, and his expression when he looked down was grim.

"We won't be needing an ambulance anymore."

Amanda felt a surge of relief wash over her body, both at being finally safe after thinking her very life was going to be slowly squeezed from her and at never having to deal with such an evil man again. Her breath was coming in ragged gasps, and she could feel the first sting of tears around the edge of her eyes as James threw a warm arm around her shoulders, pulling her toward him.

"It's okay, Amanda. It's all over."

"He...he smothered Emmett with flour at the mill and he poisoned the mayor, too! He gave her a mint after the potluck at the party, and it was poison. If you check that candy they found in the mayor's stomach, I'll bet you find that it's the same type he always has with him in his office."

James nodded in understanding. In the distance they heard the thin whine of sirens as all the police officers in the vicinity rushed to the site, and the crunch of gravel and slamming of car doors as they sped into the parking lot and hurried to help.

As James turned to the other cops crowding into the covered pier, warning them to watch their step for loose boards, Amanda realized that the murderer was now dead and that she was finally safe. The terrible mystery of how Emmet had wound up buried in her garden had now been laid to rest, and a man who had tried to kill three people and succeeded once wouldn't be hurting anyone anymore.

By the time she'd been escorted to a warm cop car and a hot cup of coffee had been pressed into her hands by a concerned-eyed policewoman, Amanda had begun to think about her neighbor. Who was he, and why was he dressed as a woman?

Maybe she should tell James, but she felt a twinge of loyalty to the disguised man. Her neighbor, whoever or whatever he was, had saved her life. Perhaps his dressing as a woman was a choice of his, but somehow

Amanda suspected that maybe his reasons for doing that had nothing to do with a lifestyle choice.

She was going to talk to her neighbor tomorrow, and get some answers, and then she'd tell James.

Chapter 31

The following day was gray and cloudy, raining again as the mist and fog crouched over the beach town. It seemed to take forever for Amanda to finally roll out of bed, groaning at the unexpected soreness throughout every muscle in her body.

Of course you're sore, she thought as she shuffled toward the bathroom medicine cabinet, in search of ibuprofen. *You were in a car accident and fought for your life.* She hadn't had much sleep, either, as the terrible events of yesterday kept playing through her mind. Over and over again she could hear that last scream from Charles, could see the wood cracking, could feel his deadly arm tight across her slim neck. In her fractured dreams she was at the police station again telling her story, signing paperwork, fighting with Charles, praying for the police to show up in time.

James must've apologized ten times to Amanda for leaving the Inn the night of the fire. At first he'd wanted to wring Robbins' neck, thinking he must've fallen asleep on the job, but after talking with the young rookie and listening to his adamant denials, he'd come to realize that Charles must've crept onto the front porch just after daybreak, and shoved the note through the mail slot after Robbins had left.

At the deposition, Amanda hadn't said a word about her 'Russian' neighbor, or to the cops she was actually a he, and that he had saved her. Maybe it was a mistake not to tell all the details of what had happened on that pier, but she felt that she owed him some sort of privacy, at least until she could talk with him.

Within fifteen minutes she was at the front door of her neighbor's small bungalow, nervously ringing the doorbell. To her surprise, Jennifer Peetman creaked open the door. Her blue eyes darted around quickly, and without a word, she grabbed Amanda's arm and suddenly pulled Amanda inside.

The room was warm and smelled of spiced tea. At the kitchen table, sitting with folded hands, was the man that Amanda had thought was Mrs. Petrovski. He was wearing the bulky clothes she'd seen him in before, when she had thought he was a woman, but had set aside the triangular headscarf.

Maybe that's why the curtains were never opened in this house, Jennifer thought as she took the seat the middle-aged man offered to her. She just had one question.

"Who *are* you?"

The man sighed, as if deeply tired. "My name is Gordon Peetman."

Jennifer nodded, cutting off Amanda's next query. "He's my father. He's been hiding here in town to be near me. I grew up here and when my dad –"

Gordon interrupted her, putting a broad hand on her forearm. "I'd been away a long time, Miss Graham, living under an assumed identity. There were a lot of reasons I couldn't come back home, but lately I've been dealing with some serious health issues, and well, I wanted to be here in Ravenwood. I wanted to spend my last days here where I was happiest, even if I had to be mostly unseen or wear a disguise to do it."

"You're sick?"

His gaze was unwavering. "The doctors say chemo would extend my life, Miss Graham, but I'm not willing to wrap up my time like that. If I have to make an exit, I'd like to have as many days where I feel good and get to be around my daughter as possible." He paused and glanced at Jennifer, who was barely holding back the tears threatening to spill over her lashes.

"I came home to die."

Amanda shifted in her chair, unsure what to say. The Peetmans both were looking at her, waiting.

"Thank you for saving my life." As soon as she said it, she could see Jennifer relax a bit, even though the girl leaned forward, intent.

"So you're not going to turn him in?"

Amanda's gaze flicked to Gordon. He was sitting quietly, obviously wanting to hear her answer.

"Why are you hiding, Mr. Peetman? And why are you scared of the police knowing about you coming back to Ravenwood Cove?"

He gestured for Jennifer to bring the teapot and once she had set it on the tablecloth and slid a plate of ginger cookies in front of Amanda, he answered her question.

"Let's just say that I used to do the books for some very unsavory characters, who really want me dead. I knew all about their dirty dealings for years, up and down the entire West coast, and they don't much like the idea of me talking to cops. You see, if you're an accountant who turns state's evidence on this group of guys, you wind up disappearing."

Amanda frowned, confused. "I thought they had witness protection programs and things like that for people who helped out the authorities."

Jennifer poured Amanda a cup of tea while Gordon explained. "They do but it's not foolproof and they definitely don't want some old bad guy going home to see his kid and to die. Too many ways the guys who didn't go to jail could find me. I didn't tell the feds when I left, because I knew they would say not to come here. They don't exactly consider Ravenwood Cove to be safe."

"As if any of this is safe!" Jennifer stood up, the anger in her voice making it shake. "You doing what you did, you coming back, you getting sick." Amanda could see the strain on the younger woman's face, and suddenly realized just how much she must've lost by having a parent who had had to stay out of her life for years.

Gordon laid a gentle hand on her arm, and slowly pulled Jennifer toward him into a hug, petting her head as she tried to gulp back her sobs of grief. Amanda watched the two of them for a moment, as the father rocked his daughter as though she was still just a little girl, comforting her.

She cleared her throat. "Why were you down on that dock?"

It took a few moments for Jennifer to pull herself out of her father's arms, and to turn back toward the stove, dabbing at her eyes. Gordon watched her for a bit, then turned back to Amanda.

"I don't get much chance to get out at all, you see, because of being dressed like I am and not being able to talk to anyone. I can't exactly pull off a Russian woman's accent," he joked humorlessly, pulling his mug of tea closer. "Some mornings, especially when it's raining and most people aren't out, I can go down the abandoned cannery really early so I can have some time to watch the ocean and think. When the tide's just right, I get a chance to gather up some mussels or clams and bring 'em back home to make seafood stew."

"He makes a great bouillabaisse. Always has," Jennifer interjected.

"Some days, that is about as normal a life as I can get, and a bowlful of seafood and getting to see my daughter is what makes my life worth living right now."

Amanda pressed him again. "Why did you help me?"

For a moment, there was a flash of anger across the man's face, and Amanda could almost see a shadow of what his younger, healthier self must've looked like.

"So, I may have worked with bad, bad men, but just because I did that doesn't mean I was one of them. I hated doing that work, but it was the only good money I could find. The more I knew, the deeper I got pulled into their world. When I saw you being dragged down that pier and heard that guy talking, I just knew he was going to kill you."

Amanda suppressed a shudder, reliving the sensation of being attacked and nearly strangled.

"You didn't deserve that. *Nobody* deserves that. I was just coming back up the ladder from getting mussels off the rocks and knew I had to do something. Didn't have a gun so I figured that my shovel would have to do."

He shifted in his chair, as if uncomfortable. "So, now my fate is in your hands, Amanda. You can turn me in to the police and they'll probably come get me and put me somewhere safe and far away from here, but I have only weeks left. I'm asking you, please don't do this."

She looked into his hopeful face, the sincerity in his eye a silent plea. It took only a moment to make the decision.

"Look, you're not doing anything illegal here in town, right? Your past is behind you?"

At his answering nod, she continued. "Then I won't tell a soul."

There was a whoop of laughter and Amanda was buried in Jennifer's over-enthusiastic hug, her arms squished at her sides while the younger woman grinned and kissed her soundly on the cheek.

"Thank you, thank you so much! I was so worried that you'd just turn him in to the cops and they'd take him away again. We need this time together..." and her voice trailed off as she finally released Amanda. "This time is precious to us."

Gordon reached over and caught Jennifer's hand. "I'm very grateful, Amanda, and you don't have to worry about me. I don't have any energy left to do anything but be a very good boy."

"Do you know that I actually followed you both once, when you drove out from your house before dawn?" They both looked surprised so she continued. "I heard your car door slam and it woke me, so I peeked outside. When I saw Jennifer with a full-sized shovel and you in the passenger seat, I thought you were both up to no good so I hopped in my car and tried to see where you were going."

Gordon's mouth was turned up in a little smile. "You mean you thought we were going to use the shovel to–" he couldn't go on, his smile cracking into a heartfelt laugh. "You thought I, I mean we, were going to bury someone?" He chuckled and wiped his eyes. "No way. I'm only good at digging clams and scraping mussels off the rocks. A heavy shovel like that works great for getting seafood."

Amanda grinned back. "Sorry. Thought you were a murderer."

"No, you thought *we* were murderers. I'm way too boring for that!" Jennifer seemed to think this was a fine joke, too. "I was just driving Dad down the pier so he could get some time out of the house and not be seen. You know, I thought I saw someone following me awhile back, but they disappeared so I thought it was no big thing."

"Guess you're just good at outrunning me."

"Guess I am! Not exactly a job skill I'll put on my resume, but it still sounds cool." Jennifer sat back down and took her father's hand gently.

He gestured toward the covered window. "I read the news in the paper today, about the changes in the city council. Last I heard the–" he began, but a coughing fit suddenly wracked his body, and Jennifer hurried to his side with a damp washcloth. He turned away from Amanda for a moment as his daughter helped him wipe his mouth, and with a shuddering breath turn back toward Amanda.

"Sorry 'bout that," he apologized, seemingly embarrassed that his illness was visible.

"What changes to the city council?"

He looked surprised and Jennifer picked up the newspaper from the kitchen counter. When she handed it to Amanda the headline leapt out at her.

MURDERER FOUND, TIMMINS DEAD

There it was, in black and white. Looking back on yesterday, and even back at the previous weeks, it sometimes still felt like some weird dream that Amanda had experienced.

The article was clear and fair, and detailed Charles' death and James' saying that the statements that Charles had made to Amanda would be taken as a confession of guilt in the murder of Emmett, and the attempted murder of Mayor Sandford. Lisa had also given all the information about the pending real estate deal with the retirement resort company, and the mayor's involvement.

That news alone was enough to shake up a small beach town, but there was more. After being confronted about her relationship with the development company, Mayor Sandford had given her resignation, and the other two council members had instantly followed suit. George Ortiz had stepped in and appointed three new members to the council temporarily, and had announced that there would be an election organized in the next few weeks to elect new city officials.

The more she read, the more exuberant Amanda became. "A whole new council! Do you know what that means? I'll bet that I can do something about that zoning now, and get the Inn back up and running!" She grinned at the Peetmans, joy evident in every line of her smile. "If I can make it work, I'm going to throw the biggest grand opening party this little town has ever seen, and you're both invited."

Gordon smiled at her, leaning his head back on his chair. "I'm sorry I won't be there to see it. Even if I'm not...even if I'm still here, you can't exactly explain why your Russian neighbor has five o'clock shadow, can you?"

Amanda laughed gently, agreeing. "Maybe not, but you should know that you'd always be welcome. Anyone who saved my life by whacking some crazy guy with a shovel gets to eat his weight in hors d'oeuvres at my place whenever he feels like it. Maybe we'll just have to arrange a time to meet after dark so I can get a taste of your famous seafood stew."

Gordon smiled, his eyes happy even if his body was tired. "Deal.

Chapter 32

The chocolate chip cookies were hot and gooey, straight out of the oven. Amanda expertly scooped several off the sheet pan and slid them onto small plates, sliding them in front of her appreciative audience. Lisa and Meg were perched on tall stools at the huge marble kitchen island, with Oscar overseeing everything from a nearby chair.

"Is this how you celebrate?" Lisa asked, pouring mugs of coffee for the trio.

"Yes, I'm a wild one. Cookies for everyone! All the fun, none of the hangover." She gestured with her turner. "Careful; they're hot."

There was a loud knock on the door and Amanda hurried to the foyer, still wearing her apron. She could see James smiling through the cut glass in the front door, and Amanda smiled back as she pulled the door open.

"Well, Detective Landon. Can't imagine why you're here today."

At her gestured invitation he stepped inside. "Yeah, not like anything's been going on in Ravenwood lately." His expression became serious. "Do I smell cookies?" and without waiting for an answer, turned and followed his nose into the kitchen. The girls greeted him and he sat down on an empty stool, obviously next in line for a plate.

Once he had his snack and a cup of coffee in front of him, he cleared his throat and dug into his coat pocket, pulling out a folded piece of paper.

"I brought you a present."

Amanda's eyebrows went up, surprised, but she took the paper and slowly unfolded it.

"It's the business license for the Inn. I wanted you to know right away that as of this morning, they've voted to rescind the ruling for long-term rentals only. That means that the Ravenwood Inn will be able to open as a bed and breakfast again, whenever you're ready."

There was a general squeal of excitement and Amanda impulsively put her arms around Lisa's neck and hugged her, exuberant. "I can't believe it! All this time of fighting to get the Inn open and now it's going to happen! I'm so excited..."

She wasn't going to cry. Really she wasn't. Well, maybe just a little happy cry. She pulled back and sniffled, trying to control herself.

James gave her the time to work out her emotions, patiently waiting as he took a bite into the warm cookie.

"The new city council rezoned you. They've also passed a resolution to reject any proposals for development from the Crown Crescent Company."

Amanda took a shuddering breath, calming herself, and carefully put the business license in a nearby desk drawer.

"I'm sorry for the waterworks. I'm just so happy that it's finally been resolved." Her eyebrows furrowed together and she turned toward James. "Everything's done with the case, I mean, about Emmett and Charles?"

The tall detective nodded, an expression of satisfaction on his face. "Yes, finally. After your deposition yesterday I investigated all the comments Charles made about manipulating legal records and blackmail and we've been able to piece everything together."

The women waited, expectant, as James laid it all out.

"So, we learned that Emmett was blackmailing him because he knew Charles had tampered with evidence in a previous case, and that if the information ever came out Charles' career would be over and he'd be going to prison." He took another bite of his gooey cookie and continued.

"As far as we can tell, the blackmail was going on for about a year and was bankrupting Charles. We know he killed Emmett by luring him up to his family's flour mill and then somehow getting him in a bin where he was able to dump flour on him, enough to suffocate him. Seems like he used the public argument Emmett and your uncle"-- James gestured at Amanda-- "had as an opportunity to kill Emmett. That way Charles could get your uncle out of the way so he could wrangle control of the Inn. The problem was that Conrad and Judy had never made a will with Charles as their lawyer."

Amanda sat down, her mind whirling as the answers were laid out in front of her. James watched her absorb all the information, and decided to tell her everything.

"He couldn't find out who they had as an heir, because there was no info about them having any kids, and since your uncle continued to pay the taxes on the Inn and it was clear of any mortgage, it never came up for a public sale or auction."

James caught Amanda's eye. "So, he had to wait for you to either abandon the place, sell the place...or...."

Amanda finished for him. "Or for me to die, since he had so many of my legal papers and written proof that he was my lawyer. He could just make up anything he wanted, forge my signature, and get control of the Inn."

They sat in silence, digesting all the information, and realizing just how closed Amanda had come to being killed.

"All for a piece of land."

James sighed. "Wars have been fought for less."

Lisa leaned forward, her face reflecting deep concentration. "So, was the mayor involved with Charles in any way?"

James shook his head. "We don't think so. Going through all of Charles' files we found a record of a meeting he had with the mayor eight years ago, where they discussed possible long-term development of the bluff part of town. We think he just got wind of a possible business dealing that could make him millions, and was willing to do whatever it took to make that happen."

"But the mayor put in the request for the zoning change, right?"

"No, actually she didn't. I checked the card file myself and interviewed the clerk at the assessor's office. She didn't remember the mayor coming in, but she did remember seeing Charles back in the files. The signature's off, too, so we think Charles forged it so he could look blameless. That way he could still be able to try to manipulate circumstances enough to get the Inn."

"Maybe I owe her an apology." Fair was fair, and if Amanda had made a mistake in judging Mrs. Sandford too harshly, she was willing to eat some crow and try to make amends.

James shrugged. "You can apologize if you want, but you should know that she was the one who set all those inspectors on you. "

So much for making amends. James could see the frustration in every line of Amanda's face. "She may have tried to sink you, Amanda, but she wasn't able to do it, was she? You fought for this Inn-" he said, pointing at Amanda emphatically, "and you won. You've helped a lot of people in this town, lady, and none of us are ever going to forget it."

She glanced up and caught his eye. "And I never will, too."

Epilogue

The scent from the huge bouquet of white roses gave a soft perfume to the elegant front hall of the historic inn, welcoming townspeople at last at the Grand Opening party.

It had taken Amanda weeks of preparation to ensure that every detail of the re-opening of the Ravenwood Inn was perfect, from the trays of delicious hors d'oeuvres to the fat pillar candles lighting the front windows. The weather had cooperated for once, with almost no breeze and a dark sky brilliant with bright stars. Even the moon was a lantern, full and fat to light the way toward the open front doors. Guests coming up the wide walkways could hear the laughter and music from the moment they parked their cars, and hurried toward Ravenwood Cove's party of the year.

Inside, the newly-restored hardwood floors and freshly-painted walls reflected the golden light of chandeliers and lamps. Ropes of ribbon and flowers looped through the main banister, and tray after tray of delicious food kept coming from the kitchen, carried by waiters specially hired for the occasion.

Amanda circulated among her guests, chatting easily and offering drinks and snacks as her new friends helped her celebrate. People had been arriving for the last half hour, exclaiming at how they loved the ragtime and Dixieland music playing in the background, and noting how beautiful the Inn looked, all decorated and full of partygoers.

It was wonderful to know so many people. The crowd was a fun mix of neighbors, friends and merchants. Most of the shop owners Amanda had helped had shown up for the open house, some bringing bottles of their favorite wine as housewarming gifts. She'd accepted their gifts with surprise and gratitude, happy to add them to her growing wine cellar.

Amanda knew she wouldn't see her neighbor, Gordon, dressing up in his Russian outfit to come eat canapes, but she greeted Jennifer warmly when she arrived, nodding to Amanda in shy greeting as Roy took her coat.

Even the ex-mayor, now just Mrs. Sandford, had turned up for the evening, carrying a gift of an expensive bottle of burgundy. Amanda made a point to greet her and thank her for the gift, and when she offered the elegant lady a cocktail it was quietly accepted. Amanda hadn't forgotten what machinations had happened to try to shut her business down, but she realized that she was going to be around the people of Ravenwood Cove for a long time, and that included the ex-mayor. It was time to build some bridges, or at least patch some broken walls.

Meg had recently joined some online dating service and had brought a date, a thin blonde fellow in a green sweater who looked like he'd rather be somewhere much more quiet. She seemed smugly proud of her new toy, and having the time of her life. Meg held his hand and dragged him from conversation to conversation, and he was enough of a good sport to let her repeatedly introduce him to so many people.

Through the open kitchen doorway, Amanda could see a lot of the partygoers, even as she circulated back to get more drinks. Mrs. Granger was sitting in the big wingback chair tucked into the corner of the main parlor, looking like a queen, a festive red bow tied to the handgrip of her nearby walker. She was holding court by telling several rapt partygoers stories about the wild history of the Ravenwood Inn, her gnarled little hands gesturing wildly to punctuate her tale. Amanda wasn't sure how many of the outrageous stories were true, but she made a mental note to do some more research on the Inn's past.

Her heart was full of gratitude as she scanned the crowd. There were so many people here who had helped her make this evening happen. Lisa, the reporter, was laughing over a glass of wine, and flirting outrageously with one of the James' younger brothers, Ethan. He definitely looked more than interested, his hand propping him up on the doorway as he leaned toward her. Meg had been an absolute trooper, helping with all the food and setup, and only leaving to pick up her grandmother and her date for the party. George Ortiz had brought his entire family, his four children only too happy to slide down the wooden banister on the back stairway again and again, all under the watchful eye of their mother, Amy.

Amanda was just ducking into the kitchen for another tray of petit fours when she saw James come through the front door with a very pregnant, very pretty blonde woman on his arm. He smiled and nodded at Amanda, as he escorted the lady toward her.

Amanda tried to keep her face neutral but a thousand questions were whirling in her head. Who was the pregnant lady with the deep blue eyes, and why was she hanging on James' arm?

"Amanda, I'd like to you to meet my sister, Christy Donovan. Christy, this is Amanda Graham."

It was amazing how the relief washed over Amanda with the simple knowledge that her handsome detective friend was escorting his sister, not his lover. Her grin may have been a bit too big, her handshake a bit too hearty, as she introduced herself to Christy. James' sister smiled warmly and shook Amanda's hand while James rocked on his heels and grinned, seemingly smug that'd he'd introduced the two ladies. Christy gestured to the decorated foyer. "What an incredible building! I can already imagine how beautiful it will be when you decorate for the holidays this year." Amanda nodded, happily agreeing. She'd discovered several boxes of vintage Christmas decorations among the boxes stored in the attic and had been itching to pull them out. "Thank you! I've been thinking the same thing, actually. This first Christmas in Ravenwood Cove will be very special for me."

James leaned forward so Amanda could hear him over the burst of laughter from a group of teenagers nearby. "Christy's in town for a few days with her husband, and they were going to stay at my folks' ranch but there's a water leak on the upper floor that made their room unlivable. I know it's short notice, but I wondered if you had any rooms available?"

A fellow with dark auburn hair came bounding up to the front desk, holding two overnight bags, and

James quickly introduced him as his brother-in-law, Rick.

"I happen to have every room vacant tonight, Detective, and I'd be happy to put your sister in our most spacious guest suite. You'll be my first," she admitted, smiling at Christy as she typed in her computer, and slid the leather bound guest register over for their signatures. Amanda couldn't suppress a thrill at the idea of having her very first guests sleep in the Inn on such a special night.

Once everything was logged and signed, Amanda led them upstairs, with James and Rick each carrying a suitcase.

"So, after all you've been through, Amanda, it hasn't been that bad, has it?"

The laugh began at her toes and bubbled out of her mouth, as free as the relief that had washed over her. She looked out at her happy partygoers, her new neighbors and friends, and the happiness, for once, was real.

"Everything I've gone through has led me here, to tonight. This is what I wanted my life to be."

Amanda jumped a bit when she felt James' hand gently touch the small of her back as they climbed the staircase to show his sister and her husband to their room. Amanda shivered, the sensation of the warmth of his broad palm on her spine so natural, so good that she didn't want it to move away.

Not a boyfriend, but maybe *something* someday.

"Well, you don't have to worry about anyone else being buried in your garden at least. That must be a relief."

She laughed and agreed. "I could stand with some quiet while I get the Inn and the business up and running. I've had so much interest from the website that I'm going to be pretty busy."

"Looks like it's up and running just fine." The sounds of laughter and Dixieland jazz floated up the stairs as Amanda looked down on the happy crowd. Not a cobweb or drifting ghost in sight.

"Besides, what else could happen in this little town?"

James turned toward her, a definite twinkle in his eye. "Have you *met* all your neighbors? This town is full of weird secrets."

Even though the room was warm, Amanda shivered with excitement. "I can't wait."

***

AUTHOR NOTES:

Wow! That was fun to write, and I hope you enjoyed it, too! If you liked what you read, **please consider leaving a review.** Being an independent author means this is my own small business, and I appreciate any feedback you can give, so other readers will know of my writing is their cup of tea or not ☺ Thank you for stopping by!

My author website is at http://CarolynDeanBooks.com/ You can see what's new there, and if you'd like to be informed about what's NEW or FREE you can sign up for my newsletter. It's spam-free, I PROMISE.

ABOUT THE AUTHOR – Carolyn L. Dean

I've been writing and making stories in my head as early as I can remember. In third grade I came home, set my lunchbox down, and told my mother I wanted to be a writer. Luckily, Mom was supportive.

I've been a published author for a few years now, under different names and genres, but the thought of writing about a small coastal town in Oregon, and about its loves and mysteries and holidays and people has been with me for years. To be honest, I am a bit scared to dump those ideas onto the written page, but hope you'll enjoy getting to meet the people who inhabit my imagination.

In real life, I'm married with kids, live on the West Coast of the US, and own a hobby farm just outside of my favorite small town. I love to travel, and can often be found strolling down a windy beach, holding onto the string of a high-sailing dragon kite.

CUPPA'S 'TO DIE FOR' CINNAMON ROLLS

Did the description of Cuppa's amazing cinnamon rolls make your mouth water? Every time I described them in this book I thought about my family's favorite recipe for cinnamon rolls, and I've included it here for you. I think Tory and Meg would approve.

All measurements/temperatures are in US units.
Makes 12 wonderfully large rolls

Dough:

> 2 packages active dry yeast
> 1 cup warm water
> 2/3 cup plus 1 teaspoon granulated sugar, divided
> 1 cup warmed milk (I microwave this and then stir to be sure there are no hot spots)
> 2/3 cup softened butter
> 2 teaspoons salt
> 2 eggs, beaten
> 7 to 8 cups all-purpose flour

Filling of Deliciousness:

> 1 cup melted butter, divided (that's 2 sticks)
> 1-3/4 cups dark brown sugar, divided
> 3 Tablespoons ground cinnamon
> 1 teaspoon ground nutmeg (fresh, if possible)
> 1 to 2 cups chopped pecans (optional)
> 1-1/2 cups dark raisins (optional)

Frosting:

> 1/2 cup melted butter

3 cups powdered sugar
1 and a half teaspoons real vanilla
5 to 8 Tablespoons hot water

DIRECTIONS:

To make dough combine yeast, warm water and 1 teaspoon sugar in a cup and stir. Set aside.

In a large bowl mix warmed milk, remaining 2/3 cup sugar, butter, salt, and eggs. Stir well and add yeast mixture. Add half the flour and beat until smooth. Stir in enough of the remaining flour to make a slightly stiff dough. It's okay for the dough to be sticky.

Turn out onto a well-floured board and knead for 5 to 10 minutes.

Place in a well-buttered glass bowl. Cover loosely and let rise in a warm draft-free place until doubled in bulk, about 1 to 1-1/2 hours.

When doubled, punch down dough and let it rest for 5 minutes. Roll out onto floured surface into a 15 x 20-inch rectangle.

Filling: Spread dough with ½ cup melted butter. Mix together 1/-1/2 cups brown sugar, cinnamon, and nutmeg. Sprinkle over buttered dough. Sprinkle with pecans and raisins, if you want. Sometimes I go really crazy and add a cup of finely-chopped apples, too.

Roll up jellyroll-fashion and pinch the edges together to seal. Cut into 12 slices. Coat bottom of a

13"x 9" and a square 8" pan with the last ½ cup of melted butter, and sprinkle remaining ¼ cup of sugar mixture on top. Place slices close together in pans. Let rise in warm, draft-free place until doubled in bulk (about 45 minutes).

Preheat oven to 350 degrees. Bake for 25 to 30 minutes, until nicely browned. Let cool slightly and spread with frosting. Share with others, and be prepared to get marriage proposals ;)

Frosting: Mix melted butter, powdered sugar, and vanilla. Add hot water a tablespoon at a time, mixing after each, until frosting is of desired consistency. Spread or drizzle over slightly-cooled rolls.

CPSIA information can be obtained
at www.ICGtesting.com
Printed in the USA
FSOW02n1558151216
28615FS

9 781539 868125